I0557823

The Moksha Vriksha

FIRST EDITION

GUIDED BY: NITKA MARGA

SoulBound BOOKS

Copyright © 2023 by Nitka Marga

All rights reserved. No part of this publication may be reproduced, distributed, or transmitted in any form or by any means, including photocopying, recording, or other electronic or mechanical methods, without the prior written permission of the publisher, except in the case of brief quotations embodied in critical reviews and certain other noncommercial uses permitted by copyright law.

This is a work of fiction. Names, characters, places, and incidents are the product of the author's imagination or are used fictitiously. Any resemblance to actual persons, living or dead, events, or is entirely coincidental.

While this story may allude to certain philosophical and spiritual concepts, it is important to note that the characters and events portrayed are entirely fictional. Any resemblance to historical figures, religious texts, or philosophical teachings is purely coincidental.

All illustrations used in this book are created with elements from Canva, a graphic design tool. The images are modified and combined to fit the context of the story. The license for the elements used in the illustrations has been obtained from Canva, and their usage complies with Canva's terms of service and license agreement.

Every effort has been made to ensure the accuracy of the information presented in this book. However, the author and the publisher assume no responsibility for errors or omissions, or for any consequences arising from the use of the information contained herein.

Cover design: SoulBound Books

Interior layout: SouldBound Books

Illustrations: Created with elements from Canva

For permission requests, please contact the publisher at www.soulboundbooksinfo.com

Printed and bound by Amazon KDP.

ISBN: 979-8-9891265-4-5

Acknowledgment

As the author of this book, I wish to share a unique aspect of its creation. In the crafting of this story, I have embraced the use of artificial intelligence as a significant assisting tool. We live in an era marked by rapid technological advancements, a landscape brimming with both opportunities and uncertainties. As a self-publishing author and a hobbyist writer, navigating this evolving terrain has been a journey of both challenges and discoveries.

I believe in transparency and, therefore, want to express that AI has significantly aided in the creation of this book. However, it's essential to clarify that AI did not independently generate this work. It served as a collaborator, enhancing my ideas and contributing to the development process. The core of the story — its heart and soul — emerged from human creativity, imagination, and lessons learned, guided by teachers and experiences.

Writing, before the advent of AI, was a journey marked by solitude, filled with the nuances of creativity, criticism, and fulfillment. These elements have remained a constant, even as AI has woven itself into the fabric of my writing process. The pride in crafting a narrative, the diligence in revision, and the sense of accomplishment upon completion have continued unabated in this AI-assisted endeavor.

I am deeply thankful for the assistance AI has provided. It has not only expanded my capabilities to publish but also enriched the experience for my readers. This novel is a testament to the beautiful synergy between human creativity and the frontiers of technological innovation.

Thank you, dear reader, for joining me on this extraordinary journey. Your engagement and support are invaluable to me, and I hope this story resonates with you as profoundly as it has with me.

With heartfelt gratitude,
Nitka Marga

The Moksha Vriksha

GUIDED BY: NITKA MARGA

PART ONE: EMBARKING ON THE TAPESTRY

PART TWO: THE REFUGE OF INNER STILLNESS

PART THREE: TRAVERSING THE WINDING PATH

"Embrace the Journey Within"

This book is lovingly dedicated to Sheena, my cherished four-legged companion. Sheena has been a source of healing, supporting me through injuries of the body, soul, and mind. Her unwavering presence and unconditional love have guided me on a path of self-understanding and evolution. Together, we have forged a bond that transcends words—a connection that has shaped me in ways I never thought possible.

Sheena, your unwavering companionship has been a catalyst for growth, instilling in me deep values of love, patience, and finding joy in every step we take together.

Part 1

Embarking on
The Tapestry

.

PART ONE - PROLOGUE
Go Forth,
Brave Seeker

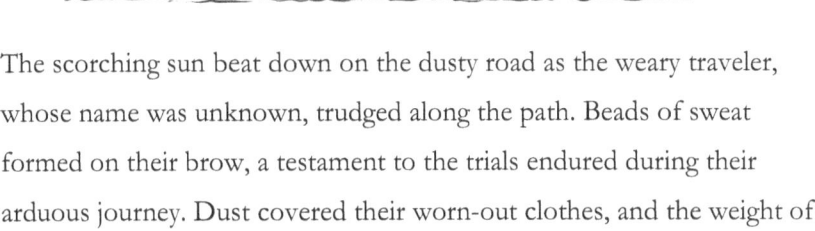

The scorching sun beat down on the dusty road as the weary traveler, whose name was unknown, trudged along the path. Beads of sweat formed on their brow, a testament to the trials endured during their arduous journey. Dust covered their worn-out clothes, and the weight of the world seemed to rest upon their shoulders.

As the traveler walked, their eyes caught sight of a figure sitting beneath the shade of a sprawling neem tree. The person, Jai, seemed lost in thought, their gaze fixed on the distant horizon. Jai's face mirrored the weariness etched in the traveler's own features. It was as if they shared an unspoken connection, a recognition of the struggles that life can impose.

Approaching with cautious steps, the traveler's curiosity sparked an unspoken conversation between them and Jai. The traveler took a seat on a weathered rock beside Jai. The air hung heavy with unspoken words, as if waiting for the right moment to be released.

Finally, Jai turned their head towards the traveler and acknowledge their presence. There was a depth to Jai's gaze, as if they carried the weight of their own struggles and the collective burden of the world's sorrows.

In that fleeting moment, the traveler sensed a shared understanding between them. Without uttering a single word, they recognized the battles

1

fought within each other's souls. It was a meeting of kindred spirits, two wanderers searching for solace and meaning.

Jai broke the silence, their voice gentle yet tinged with the weariness of a thousand sleepless nights. "You look burdened, my friend," they said, their voice carrying the weight of empathy. "The journey has not been kind to you, I see."

The traveler nodded, their eyes reflecting a mix of pain and hope. "Indeed, the road has been treacherous," they replied, their voice echoing with both longing and determination. "I seek something, something that can heal the wounds that reside within."

Jai's gaze softened; their face etched with understanding. "We are all travelers on this path of life, burdened by our own battles," they murmured, the weight of their words carried by the wind. They paused for a moment, as if reflecting on the vast tapestry of human existence.

With a gentle smile, Jai began to speak, their voice a melodious caress that enraptured the listener's senses. They spun a tale of enchantment and wonder, a tapestry woven with threads of ancient wisdom and hidden truths. Jai spoke of the fabled Moksha Vriksha, a mystical tree said to hold the secrets of profound healing, and the key to enlightenment. Each word they uttered resonated with the collective yearning for transformation, the universal longing to find solace amidst life's hardships.

"In the realms of existence," Jai continued, their voice now carrying the weight of countless stories, "we are but wanderers seeking solace, searching for a balm to soothe the wounds of our journey. The Moksha Vriksha beckons to us all, offering the promise of renewal and restoration."

The traveler's eyes shimmered with curiosity as they leaned closer to Jai. "Where can I find this sacred Moksha Vriksha?" they whispered, their voice filled with anticipation and a tinge of longing.

"Listen closely, my dear traveler," Jai whispered, their voice a lullaby that danced upon the air. "The Moksha Vriksha stands at the heart of a labyrinthine journey, a pilgrimage of the soul. It is a path that transcends the boundaries of time and space, leading seekers toward their own rebirth."

The traveler's eyes widened, captivated by the shimmering visions painted by Jai's words. They felt the stirrings of a dormant yearning, a thirst for transformation that had long slumbered within. The promise of the Moksha Vriksha beckoned, a distant siren's call that tugged at the depths of their being.

Jai's voice carried the weight of experience, each syllable laden with the trials and triumphs of their own odyssey. "Know this, traveler, the path to the tree is not for the faint of heart. It demands courage to confront your fears, resilience to weather the storms, and unwavering faith to guide you through the darkest hours."

The traveler's heart quickened, its rhythm aligning with the pulse of the journey that awaited. They dared to imagine the winding paths, the treacherous terrain, and the whispers of ancient secrets that would accompany their every step. The yearning within bloomed into resolute determination, a flame that could not be extinguished.

"Thank you, Jai," the traveler spoke with heartfelt gratitude. "Your words have ignited a fire within me, and I am ready to embark on this sacred quest to the Moksha Vriksha. May our paths cross again when my journey reaches its culmination."

Jai nodded, a wise smile gracing their lips. "Go forth, brave seeker," they whispered, their voice carrying the weight of untold stories. "May the winds of destiny guide you, and may the tree reveal its secrets to you when the time is ripe."

Jai looked towards the sun, a touch of melancholy in their gaze. "As my beloved often said, 'Every sunset promises a sunrise...'," they began, their voice trailing off, leaving the traveler to ponder on the unsaid words and the journey that lay ahead.

With a final glance back, the traveler set their gaze forward, their footsteps resolute as they ventured into the unknown. The echoes of Jai's wisdom lingered in their heart, fueling their determination to face the trials that awaited. In the realms of storytelling, the threads of their destinies intertwined, as the story of Jai's own journey unraveled, waiting to be discovered in the chapters that lay ahead.

The traveler embarked on their odyssey, guided by the whispers of ancient tales and the flickering light of hope. The path stretched before them, illuminated by the promise of transformation and renewal. They would navigate through darkness and embrace the challenges that tested their spirit, for deep within, they carried the knowledge that true healing awaited, intricately woven into the fabric of the journey itself.

PART ONE - CHAPTER ONE
Whispers of Longing: Echoes of Loss

"Compassion is the foundation of non-violence; truthfulness is the essence of authenticity; non-stealing honors the sacredness of abundance; moderation nurtures harmony; non-possessiveness reveals the freedom of letting go."

- Unknown

As the sun began to set, painting the sky with golden hues, time itself seemed to shift, transporting us back to a moment before Jai embarked on their journey to the Moksha Vriksha. In this intricately woven narrative of the past, we find ourselves in the vibrant city of Mohendrapur, where Jai, a pilgrim of destiny, seeks solace in their makeshift shelter.

In the tapestry of Jai's existence, many nights were spent in makeshift shelters scattered across various corners of the city. Yet, on this particular night, as if orchestrated by a cosmic symphony, their journey took on a newfound significance.

In this moment of reflection, Jai carefully sets up their humble tent, seeking solace amidst the ebb and flow of life's currents. The day had been filled with the rhythm of the market, as Jai diligently set up their artisan stall, meticulously arranging masterfully crafted creations. Each piece carefully arranged, spoke of a connection to creativity— a hidden artisan on a transient canvas.

As the sun descended below the horizon, Jai retreated to the sanctuary of their shelter, allowing the quietude of the night to envelop their weary form. The sounds of the bustling city slowly dissipated, replaced by the serenade of a nearby river.

In the depths of their shelter, in the sanctuary of their reflections, Jai found moments of solace in the gentle embrace of the river's melodic song.

Lying there, upon a bed of woven fabrics and soft cushions, Jai's thoughts meandered through the labyrinthine corridors of their mind. The events of the day, the vibrant faces they encountered, and the shared moments of connection flickered through their memory like the dance of a flickering flame.

Under the veiled embrace of the night, Jai felt an inexplicable ache pulsating within their being. It was a yearning born from the depths of their soul, a profound longing for release from the burdens that weighed heavily upon their heart. With a heavy sigh, Jai emerged from the shelter and made their way toward the river, seeking solace in its serene waters.

The darkness enveloped Jai like a cloak, concealing their form as they approached the water's edge. The river, an ancient witness to countless stories, flowed steadily in the moonlight, its ripples reflecting the shimmering stars above. With trembling hands, Jai dipped their fingers into the cool waters, feeling the gentle current caress their skin.

With a voice laced with vulnerability and an unwavering resolve, Jai spoke softly, their words carried by the night breeze, as if reaching out to a higher power that resided within the celestial realms. It was a prayer, an intimate conversation between Jai and the universe, a plea for liberation from the shackles of suffering that had wrapped their heart in a tight embrace.

"Oh, Divine forces that dwell within the boundless expanse of the cosmos, I stand before you, humbled and longing for solace," Jai began, their voice filled with both desperation and an unwavering hope. "In the depths of my being, I carry a burden, a heaviness that I cannot fully comprehend. It gnaws at my spirit, casting shadows upon my days and haunting the corridors of my restless nights."

The words flowed forth, carried by the raw emotions that swirled within Jai's heart. They spoke of the weariness that clung to their bones, of the questions that tugged relentlessly at the corners of their mind. "I yearn for freedom, for release from the chains that bind me. Show me the path that leads to liberation, where suffering is but a distant memory. Grant me the strength to confront the darkness within and to embrace the light that resides in the depths of my being."

With every word uttered into the night, Jai poured their anguish, their hopes, and their dreams into the cosmic expanse. They bared their soul, seeking guidance and a glimmer of understanding that might offer respite from the ceaseless ache within.

The river flowed on, its steady current carrying away Jai's words, as if offering them to the farthest reaches of the universe. And in the quietude that followed, Jai stood in contemplation, their gaze fixed upon the moon's gentle reflection upon the water's surface. In that moment, a subtle shift occurred within them, an acknowledgment that their plea had been heard, even if the answers remained veiled for now.

As the first light of dawn gently kissed the sky, Jai stirred from a deep slumber, their eyes fluttering open to the soft caress of the morning breeze. A moment of disorientation washed over them as they realized they had fallen asleep by the river's edge, their body cradled by the comforting embrace of nature.

Stretching their limbs and shaking off the remnants of sleep, Jai rose to their feet, their gaze tracing the tranquil flow of the river before them. It was in this serene sanctuary that Jai had sought solace, unaware of the transformative forces at play.

Leaving the tranquil river behind, Jai made their way back to the shelter they had called home, their steps heavy with the weight of uncertainty. As they approached the site, a sinking feeling settled deep within their chest, foreshadowing the disheartening sight that awaited them.

With each cautious step, Jai's heart sank further, their eyes scanning the scene that unfolded before them. The shelter, once a humble refuge from the world's chaos, now stood in shambles, its structure marred by the ruthless hands of intrusion. The remnants of their meager belongings were scattered about, a disarray of broken dreams and stolen treasures.

As they sifted through the wreckage, a mixture of anger and sorrow swelled within Jai. Their cherished possessions—carefully crafted items, tokens of artistry and creativity—had been callously taken.

Amidst the chaos, the gentle texture of a palm leaf touched Jai's fingers. Recognizing the delicate leaf, Jai unfurled it, catching a glimpse of the last line:

"In this world and beyond, we're destined to be,
Forever connected, in love's symphony."

Jai's gaze fell upon their now-empty satchel, a poignant symbol of the void that had been left in its wake. The satchel, once a faithful companion carrying the tools of an artist's trade, now echoed with emptiness—a hollow reminder of the tangible losses they had suffered. The weight of the theft settled upon their shoulders, threatening to crush their spirit.

The scene before them painted a picture of loss and desolation, each broken fragment serving as a painful testament to the harsh realities of their journey. A heavy sigh escaped Jai's lips as they sank to their knees, the weight of despair threatening to consume them.

With closed eyes, Jai sought solace in the darkness, a respite from the harsh reality that surrounded them. As they surrendered to the quietude of their thoughts, a gentle touch graced their shoulder, causing their eyes to flutter open in surprise. It was a young boy, the bearer of a wood carving tool, a clamp, standing before them with a look of compassion etched upon his face.

Jai accepted the tool from the boy, their fingers curling around its worn handle. In that exchange, an unspoken understanding passed between them—a recognition of the shared human experience.

As the boy faded into the shadows, Jai closed their eyes, momentarily lost in the vastness of their emotions—past losses, the immediate devastation, and the uncertainty of the future looming ahead.

PART ONE - CHAPTER TWO

A Bond Beneath the Waves

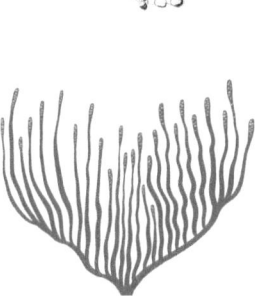

Jai, filled with a mix of sorrow and determination, gathered what was left of their belongings and prepared to embark on their search for the stolen items. The morning sun cast its warm rays on Jai as they made their way through the city to the bustling market, their mind set on finding any trace of their belongings or potential leads to the thief.

As Jai navigated through the vibrant market, their attention was drawn to a stall adorned with a colorful array of medicinal herbs and plants. Anaya, a gentle and compassionate seaweed alchemist, stood behind the stall, radiating an aura of serenity and wisdom. The aroma of ocean and the soft rustling of seaweed filled the air around her.

Approaching Anaya's stall, Jai was captivated by the beauty and tranquility that surrounded the seaweed alchemist. Anaya's eyes, filled with warmth and understanding, welcomed Jai's presence.

Jai, their voice tinged with frustration and a desperate need for answers, poured out their story of the robbery, their anger evident in every word. Anaya listened attentively, her presence calming and grounding.

After Jai finished, Anaya paused for a moment, absorbing the weight of Jai's emotions. With a soft smile, she began, "Let me take you to the magnificent depths of the ocean, where an extraordinary partnership flourished."

"In these depths, where sunlight filters through turquoise waters, lived a clownfish named Daya," Anaya recounted. "Daya observed, with both curiosity and concern, the unfortunate fate of other fish as they approached the graceful sea anemones."

"Fish, time and again, would charge at the anemones, driven by revenge and a need to retaliate against their stinging tentacles. Yet, their aggression would only result in pain as the anemones fiercely defended themselves with venom."

"In the midst of this endless cycle of hostility," Anaya continued, "Daya, a courageous and empathetic clownfish, chose a different path. He approached a solitary sea anemone with tenderness and understanding, sensing its deep-seated sorrow and the limitations of its stationary life."

"Daya recognized the anemone's longing to explore the vastness of the ocean and the wonders beyond its reach. And so, he began sharing tales of the ocean's magnificence. He painted vivid images of shimmering coral reefs, the gentle sway of seaweed, and the mesmerizing dance of sunlight on the waves."

"Each day, after his adventures, Daya would return and regale the sea anemone with stories. The once isolated and desolate creature found solace and renewed joy in Daya's tales. Through his words, he brought the vastness of the ocean alive, filling the anemone's world with wonder."

"As the days passed, their bond deepened," Anaya's voice was tender. "Daya's compassion nurtured the anemone, and in return, the anemone became Daya's protective haven amidst the reef."

"Their unique bond stood as a testament to the transformative power of empathy and understanding. Daya's decision to approach with kindness instead of aggression resulted in a profound connection, one built on mutual support."

As Anaya's story neared its end, her voice softened even further, "In the vast tapestry of nature, we see numerous examples of interconnectedness and harmony. The tale of Daya and the sea anemone is but one reminder that choosing compassion and understanding can lead to extraordinary transformations."

Before parting ways, Anaya reached beneath her stall, producing a bundle of weathered beach wood sheets. "If you're to carry the tools of an artisan," she remarked, nodding toward the clamp the boy had given Jai, "perhaps you might wish to learn the craft of creating art. These sheets, they might help you carry the memories of what you've lost."

Jai's fingers brushed the beach wood, feeling the tales they could tell. "I already know the craft," they responded quietly, a hint of pain in their eyes. "I'm a traveling artisan."

Anaya blinked in surprise, clearly not expecting this revelation. There was a silent, shared confusion between them, an unspoken question that neither had the answer to.

Moments stretched as both tried to reconcile the unexpected twist. Yet neither pressed for clarity, sensing that some stories were better left for another day. The two exchanged a mutual, understanding shrug, choosing to set aside the mystery for the moment.

With a nod of gratitude and the weight of memories pressing on their heart, Jai bid Anaya farewell. They left, carrying not just the beachwood sheets but the unspoken riddles of the day, as they continued their quest for their stolen belongings.

PART ONE -
CHAPTER THREE
Forged in Truth

Jai's footsteps echoed in the alleyways, leading them deeper into the city's core. The rhythmic clang of hammers drew them toward a blacksmith's workshop, where Kavi, a seasoned craftsman, was engrossed in his work.

The workshop was alive with energy. Sparks danced around as Kavi hammered away, and Jai approached, seeking information about their stolen possessions.

Kavi listened intently as Jai recounted their ordeal. Instead of solely blaming the thieves, Kavi encouraged Jai to reflect on their own choices. "Truthfulness goes beyond blame," Kavi said. "While the robbers played their part, one must also consider one's actions. You left your belongings unattended knowing the injustices that plague this city"

Kavi let the words linger in the air for a moment, allowing Jai to absorb the weight of his words. Breaking the brief silence, he shifted his gaze to the sheets of beach wood in Jai's satchel. "With the right touch and artistic vision," Kavi remarked, "these could become truly magnificent pieces."

"I know. I am, after all, an artist," Jai replied with pride.

Kavi's eyebrows raised in a brief moment of surprise, but he recovered quickly, offering a smile of support. "Worry not," Kavi replied, determination in his eyes. "I'll fashion you a knife for your artistic journey."

As Kavi worked, his rhythmic hammering took on a melodic cadence, accompanying his narration of the Moksha Vriksha legend.

Kavi's gaze met Jai's, sensing the depth of their emotion. There was a weight in the air, like a secret yearning to be revealed. Slowly, Kavi began, his voice gentle yet carrying a reverence, "Jai, there are moments in our lives when the universe conspires to answer our most profound calls. Today might be one such day for you."

Jai's eyes narrowed, curiosity shimmering in them. "What do you mean?"

"In ancient scriptures, whispered through generations, there exists the legend of the Moksha Vriksha, the Tree of Liberation," Kavi explained, his voice resonating with the weight of centuries. "It's said that this tree has the power to heal the deepest wounds, provide clarity to the most tangled thoughts, and offer liberation to souls burdened with worldly sorrows."

Jai leaned in, every fiber of their being attuned to Kavi's words. The tale seemed to weave around them, each word resonating with the prayer they had whispered to the cosmos.

Kavi continued, "The Moksha Vriksha doesn't just grant liberation; it aids in understanding, in transformation. Those who seek it don't just find healing; they discover their truest selves, their connection to everything."

A shiver ran down Jai's spine. Their earlier plea to the universe echoed in their ears, and here was Kavi, speaking of a possible answer. The synchronicity of it all was too significant to ignore.

"Kavi," Jai began, voice thick with emotion, "I recently sent a prayer into the vastness, seeking guidance, a sign. Your words... this Moksha Vriksha... could this be the universe's response?"

Kavi smiled warmly, nodding. "Perhaps, Jai. Sometimes the universe whispers, and at other times, it orchestrates grand tales. But always, it answers. The Moksha Vriksha may very well be the beacon guiding you towards the answers you seek."

Jai took a deep breath, the weight of their quest settling in. With newfound resolve, they whispered, "Then I must seek this tree, Kavi. For in its shade might lie the liberation my soul yearns for."

Kavi placed a reassuring hand on Jai's shoulder. "Remember, the journey to the Moksha Vriksha is as transformative as the tree itself. Embrace each step, and may you find what your heart seeks."

As Kavi held up the glimmering knife, Jai, unable to contain their admiration, said, "Your skill with engraving is truly remarkable."

Kavi gave a soft smile. "I learned much from Mata. She was an artist, unparalleled in her craft."

Jai's brows furrowed in confusion. "Mata? I've never heard of them."

Kavi's expression became more guarded, his eyes searching Jai's face. "That's how it is now, is it? Be well, Jai."

Grateful, Jai tucked the knife into their satchel, sensing its significance. With a renewed spirit, Jai ventured forth, searching for their stolen items, carrying not just the weight of the knife but the hopes and aspirations it symbolized.

As Jai journeyed on, every corner they turned held the promise of a new discovery, and within their heart, a flame of determination burned brightly.

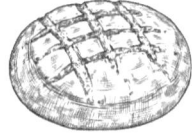

Echoes of Ethics: Secrets of the Silent Wood

Jai made their way through the bustling market; their eyes scanned the colorful stalls and vibrant crowds. The aroma of various spices and the sound of vendors hawking their goods filled the air. Hunger gnawed at Jai's belly, a constant reminder of their empty stomach.

Amidst the lively market scene, Jai's gaze fell upon a small bakery tucked away in a corner. The tantalizing display of freshly baked bread was a sight to behold. Loaves of various shapes and sizes adorned the shelves, their golden crusts glistening under the warm glow of the sun. The air around the bakery seemed to carry the irresistible scent of warm dough, wafting through the bustling crowd.

Jai's mouth watered at the sight. Their stomach grumbled in protest, aching for nourishment. Each loaf seemed to call out to them, teasing their senses with promises of satisfaction and relief. The bread appeared perfectly baked, with a crust that crackled invitingly when touched and a soft, warm center that held the promise of comfort and satiety.

As Jai's hunger grew more pronounced, their resolve weakened. They could almost taste the bread, envisioning the tender crumb melting on their tongue, providing the nourishment they so desperately craved. But deep down, a twinge of guilt tugged at their conscience, reminding them of the consequences that could follow an act of theft.

Caught in a moment of conflicting desires, Jai wrestled with their inner turmoil. The sight of the delicious bread was both a temptation and a torment, fueling their hunger and desperation. They longed to sate their appetite, to experience the simple pleasure of a warm loaf in their hands, yet they knew that taking it without permission would be a betrayal of their own principles.

As Jai's gaze lingered on the mouthwatering bread, a sudden idea sparked in their mind. They reached into their satchel and retrieved one of the small wood sheets that Anaya had given them. With the engraved knife carefully in hand, Jai swiftly carved intricate patterns onto the surface of the wood, channeling their frustration, hunger, and longing into each delicate stroke.

With careful precision, Jai seemed to carve the wooden sheet, appearing to fashion it into a beautifully crafted butter tray. Delicate patterns resembling blooming lotus flowers danced along the edges of the wood, adding a touch of grace to the rustic beauty of the butter tray.

The final strokes of the knife revealed a masterpiece—a butter tray that exuded both practicality and artistry. Jai marveled at their creation, the wooden vessel a testament to their resourcefulness and hunger-fueled ingenuity.

Approaching the baker's stall with the carved tray in hand, Jai's eyes met the baker's curious gaze. Their attention shifted from the kneading dough to the tray held tenderly by Jai. The baker's eyes traced the intricate carvings that adorned the wooden surface—designs of impeccable finesse and elegance.

"The designs..." the baker began, a tone of nostalgia in their voice, "They're strangely familiar. I remember an artisan from years past with a similar touch. Such beauty..." The baker then glanced at the words, "Moksha Vriksha," etched in a stark contrast to the elegance of the designs. The letters were carved more crudely, almost as if by a different hand.

Jai's voice carried a mixture of hunger and humility as they spoke, "In exchange for a small portion of bread, I offer you this tray. It is a humble creation of mine."

The baker's eyes continued to dance over the designs, clearly intrigued. "These patterns... they remind me of a time gone by," they mused, more to themselves than to Jai. Then, shaking off their reverie, the baker met Jai's expectant gaze, "Very well," the baker said, their voice filled with compassion.

With a sense of relief and gratitude, Jai handed over the butter tray to the baker, and in return, the baker handed them a warm loaf of bread. As Jai felt the weight of the bread in their hands, the aroma enveloping their senses, a wave of comfort washed over them.

After exchanging the tray for bread, Jai hesitated for a moment. Gathering courage, they asked, "You mentioned the Moksha Vriksha when you saw the tray. Do you know of its tales?"

Recognition continued to play in the baker's eyes, and their voice took on a gentle tone, "The Moksha Vriksha, the tree of liberation and healing. It's said to possess wondrous powers. Those words, etched so differently from the designs, they're weighty, aren't they?"

Jai's heart skipped a beat, intrigued by the baker's words. "Do you know where the tree can be found?" they asked, a glimmer of hope shining in their eyes.

The baker's smile turned wistful. "I'm afraid I don't know its exact location, my dear. The Moksha Vriksha is a rare and mystical tree, hidden deep within the realms of legends and whispers. But those who have encountered its presence speak of its healing properties and the transformative journeys it offers." Pausing for a brief moment, the baker continued with a reflective tone, "Many seek the Moksha Vriksha, hoping to find answers in its roots and solace in its branches, yet its true magic lies within the spirit of the seeker."

Bidding the baker farewell, they stepped into the teeming streets. Each stride was fueled by a resurgence of hope. The baker's words had lit a torch inside Jai's heart, pushing away the shadows of doubt that had threatened to overwhelm them.

The market around them seemed to pulse with life, each stall and face telling its own story. And as Jai wove through the crowd, the world seemed sharper, colors brighter. It was as if every detail, from the distant call of a vendor to the playful laughter of children, was drawing them deeper into the tapestry of their own journey.

A cool breeze brushed past, carrying with it the scents of spices, incense, and something more elusive — a hint of destiny. The feeling was intangible, like trying to grasp a fleeting dream upon waking. But it was there, a sense that the universe was aligning, guiding Jai's every step.

They paused for a moment, looking up. The golden sun bathed the city in its warmth, casting long shadows that danced and melded with the crowd. It was a moment of clarity, a brief interlude where everything made sense.

With the image of the Moksha Vriksha etched in their heart and the baker's words echoing in their ears, Jai continued on, each step a promise, a commitment to the journey that awaited.

PART ONE - CHAPTER FIVE

A Lost Grip

Jai walked through the bustling market, the memory of their belongings weighing heavily on their mind. The intricately designed art pieces weren't just objects; they were fragments of a past that Jai clung to, even if that attachment was shrouded in a fog of half-remembered truths.

Having eaten a portion of the bread to satisfy their hunger, Jai's energy was restored, albeit momentarily. They felt a mix of frustration and determination, fueled by the knowledge that their belongings had been taken from them. The city held the secrets of their loss, and Jai was determined to uncover them.

With every step, Jai's eyes darted from stall to stall, their heart beating with a blend of anxiety and hope. But the market remained silent, offering no clues or solace. It seemed as though the stolen items had vanished into thin air, leaving only an unsettling void in their wake.

Undeterred by the lack of leads, Jai made a decision—they would return to the place where the shelter once stood, where their journey had begun. It was a place steeped in memories and hidden truths, a starting point to retrace the path of the thieves and unravel the mystery that shrouded their stolen belongings.

As Jai retraced their steps through the winding streets, the city whispered fragments of their story—a subtle reminder of the injustice that had befallen them. The echoes of their past propelled Jai forward, igniting a fire within to seek answers amidst the remnants of their shattered sanctuary.

Jai turned the corner; their heart raced at the site where the robbery had taken place. There, within sight, sit a man with his back to Jai. Beside the man, lay Jai's cherished possessions. The sight of their belongings ignited a burning rage within Jai, fueling thoughts of retribution and violence.

In the depths of their anger, Jai instinctually reached into their satchel, feeling the cold touch of the knife gifted by the blacksmith.

As Jai approached the man, their footsteps echoed softly against the bustling backdrop of the city. The man sat hunched over, his shoulders burdened by the weight of unseen sorrows. Jai could feel their own anger simmering within, fueled by the sight of their stolen belongings lying beside him.

As Jai held the blade, the sun's rays caught the words "Moksha Vriksha." The radiant beams illuminated the intricate carvings, infusing the moment with a touch of divine luminescence.

Jai's expression softened at glance of the sun-kissed words. Their gaze shifted from the gleaming blade to the man seated before them. His posture, etched with weariness and despair.

As Jai sheathed the blade and returned it to their satchel, their fingers brushed against the smooth surface of the beach wood. A rush of memories flooded their mind—the soothing voice of the seaweed alchemist recounting the tale of Daya, the brave clownfish.

In that moment, Jai felt a profound connection to Daya's journey—a path that defied the expectations of a world entrenched in violence.

Daya's choice to embrace empathy and compassion had broken the cycle, transforming not only his own life but the life of the sea anemone, as well.

The beach wood became a tangible reminder of Daya's resilience and the transformative power of choosing a different path. It whispered of the possibility of healing, redemption, and the capacity to create ripples of change through acts of kindness and understanding.

In the presence of the man who held their stolen belongings, Jai allowed the echoes of Daya's story to guide their actions. They sat beside him, no longer driven by anger or revenge, but by the yearning for connection and the belief in the inherent goodness of humanity.

Jai settled themselves next to the man, the weight of their stolen belongings between them. The man, initially perplexed by Jai's presence, soon realized the truth as Jai calmly revealed that these items rightfully belonged to them. Confusion danced in the man's eyes, quickly replaced by a mix of guilt and remorse.

"Why did you take my possessions?" Jai's voice quivered with a mix of anger and curiosity. They needed to understand the motive behind this act of theft.

The man's face contorted, and he dropped to his hands and knees, bowing before Jai. His voice trembled as he pleaded for forgiveness. Between desperate gasps for air, he managed to explain that it was not he who had committed the act, but his two sons.

With a heavy heart, the man called out to the boys who had been playing by the river, unaware of the unfolding situation. The boys approached hesitantly, their gaze fixed on the ground, fully aware of the gravity of their actions.

Jai's eyes met the elder boy's, a mix of disappointment and understanding evident in their gaze.

"Why did you take my possessions?" Jai's voice softened; the anger replaced by a genuine desire to comprehend their motivations.

The boy's voice quivered as he explained their desperate circumstances, the hardships they faced in a world that often turned a blind eye to their struggles. It was not greed that drove them, but the desperate need for survival.

Driven by the desperation to secure food, the boy's young heart was willing to resort to theft, seizing any item that held the potential for profit. In the delicate beauty of Jai's artistic creations, he saw an opportunity—a means to acquire the resources his family desperately needed.

In that moment, Jai saw their own reflection in the boy's eyes— a glimpse of understanding of the unjust nature of the world and the lengths one might go to secure their existence. The anger dissipated, replaced by a profound empathy for the boy and his family.

As the words hung in the air, forgiveness began to weave its gentle threads. Jai extended a hand to the boy, a gesture of reconciliation and compassion. The boy accepted, tears streaming down his face, and the weight of guilt slowly lifting from his young shoulders.

In this shared moment of vulnerability and forgiveness, a new understanding bloomed. The journey for Jai's stolen belongings had led them not only to the truth of their own resilience but also to a recognition of the complex tapestry of humanity.

The father, understanding the depth of Jai's forgiveness and compassion, turned to his sons and firmly instructed them to give back Jai's belongings. The boys, realizing the gravity of their actions, handed over the stolen items to Jai.

26

But as Jai held their possessions in their hands, a moment of contemplation washed over them. With a serene smile, Jai looked at the boys and said, "You may keep what you took from me. Take what you can to the market and use the earnings to fill your bellies," Jai spoke with a gentle but firm voice. "And if you are willing, be courageous enough to pick up my tools and create something of your own. Your creations can be sold too, paving a new path for yourselves."

The boys exchanged bewildered glances, their expressions a mixture of astonishment and gratitude. They couldn't believe Jai's generosity, offering them not only forgiveness but also an opportunity to change their lives for the better.

The father, moved by Jai's words, placed a hand on each of his sons' shoulders, conveying his appreciation for the unexpected chance they had been given. It was a chance to leave behind the path of theft and embrace a path of creativity and self-sufficiency.

The father, overwhelmed with gratitude, began to express his heartfelt thanks to Jai for the unexpected act of kindness. But before he could utter the words, Jai gently interrupted him, a solemn expression on their face.

"Please understand," Jai interjected, their voice filled with determination, "I am not doing this for you and your boys alone. I am doing it for myself as well. I have a journey ahead of me, a quest to find the Moksha Vriksha, and I must travel light. Carrying the weight of my belongings will only impede my progress."

The father's eyes widened in astonishment, a mix of admiration and understanding filling his gaze. He realized that Jai's act of generosity extended beyond their immediate circumstances. It was driven by a deep sense of purpose, a burning desire to pursue a greater truth and healing.

With a nod of acknowledgment, the father lowered his gaze and offered a heartfelt gratitude that transcended mere words. He understood that Jai's quest for the Moksha Vriksha was not just about finding a legendary tree but about finding one's own liberation and enlightenment.

With the weight of their shared understanding, Jai bid the father and his boys farewell, leaving behind a moment of profound connection. The path lay before them, diverging in different directions, but the impact of their encounter would forever remain etched in their hearts.

As Jai moved forward in their journey, the deeper layers of their decision began to unfold, not entirely grasped but profoundly felt. Letting go of the art pieces was more than just a release of material possessions; it was the beginning of untangling a complex tapestry from their past, embracing what lay ahead even amidst the haze of obscured memories.

PART ONE – CHAPTER SIX

The Seductive Veil: Temptation and Transcendence

After several days of fruitless inquiries and relentless searching, Jai's determination to find the path to the Moksha Vriksha remained unyielding. The bustling city had offered no leads, no whispers of guidance, leaving Jai feeling disheartened and lost amidst the crowded streets.

Exhaustion gnawed at their bones as hunger pangs intensified, reminding Jai of the dire need to replenish their body. With weariness etched across their face, Jai made their way back to the familiar forge of Kavi, the blacksmith who had once bestowed the engraved knife upon them.

As Jai approached the smithy, the rhythmic clanging of hammers against metal reverberated through the air, signaling Kavi's industrious presence.

The blacksmith's eyes met Jai's, a mixture of recognition and concern flickering within them. With a voice revealing both hope and despair, Jai shared the tale of their futile search and the emptiness that was beginning to consume them. Kavi listened with patience, the rhythmic hammering pausing for the moment.

Kavi, with his voice filled with empathy and wisdom, said, "Perhaps what you seek is not in the streets or tales of old, but in the hidden corridors of the soul and dreams."

Intrigued and desperate for insight, Jai focused intently on Kavi's every word. As twilight approached, Kavi revealed a vial containing a swirling, iridescent liquid. "This elixir," Kavi began, "offers clarity and insight, a chance to see beyond the ordinary."

The promise of the potion, paired with Kavi's infectious energy, ignited a spark in Jai. The daunting task of finding the Moksha Vriksha momentarily faded as they decided to share the mysterious concoction.

Imbibing the elixir, reality seemed to shift. An overwhelming sense of euphoria swept over them, and the world transformed into vibrant colors and patterns. The two sang:

In the land of ancient tales, where dreams converge,
We dance and sway, as our desires surge.
Under the canopy of the starry embrace,
Together in euphoria, our spirits race.

Oh, raise your cup, to the mysteries untold,
In the golden haze, watch the night unfold.
With laughter and song, our souls take flight,
Lost in the fervor, under the moon's soft light.

Echoes of legends, in the air they sing,
As passion and elation, to our hearts they cling.
In this ancient dance, of dreams and chase,
We seek the Vriksha, in its sacred space.

So, raise your cup, let the elixir flow,
In the realm of wonder, let your spirit glow.
As dawn's embrace nears, and shadows flee,
Our quest continues, for the sacred tree.

In the midst of the altered state, two ethereal beings emerged, their presence radiant and almost otherworldly. Their every movement seemed choreographed by the cosmos, exuding an allure that was both tantalizing and mystic. Kavi, wholly entranced by one of them, seemed to drift away, following the creature into a dance of his own, leaving Jai and the other being in a poignant face-off.

The being moved closer to Jai, their eyes locking in an intimate embrace. Within those depths, Jai felt an overwhelming sense of recognition, a profound connection that resonated beyond time and space. It felt as if the being was reaching out, not just physically, but spiritually, attempting to pull Jai into a dance of souls.

The atmosphere around them grew thick with intensity. Every gesture from the being hinted at an invitation to experience a connection of profound sensuality and depth. The promise of unparalleled ecstasy lingered tantalizingly in the air.

However, within Jai's eyes, a battle raged. The allure of the being was undeniable, and the temptation immense. But as they stood at the precipice of surrender, a deep-rooted fidelity stirred, acting as an anchor. A memory of a bond, a commitment that held them back from the edge of desire.

Summoning a strength born from deep within, Jai's voice, gentle yet firm, began to convey their feelings. They alluded to an existing bond, one that transcended the present moment—a connection that was far deeper, more sacred, and could not be set aside, even in the face of such overwhelming temptation.

The weight of Jai's words and their decision to remain true to an unspoken commitment left a tangible impact, causing a momentary pause in the room's atmosphere. The being, sensing Jai's steadfast resolution, withdrew gracefully, even as the lingering echoes of the encounter resonated in the heart of both.

As dawn's first light filtered in, Jai awoke with a new energy. The vivid memories of the night before seemed to fade into mere illusions. The urgency of the quest weighed heavily on Jai's heart.

Seeing Kavi still lost in the remnants of the elixir's trance, a sharp realization hit Jai. Kavi's lack of initiative and the shadows in his eyes hinted at a deeper struggle. The quest for Moksha Vriksha, once a united ambition, now seemed distant and divergent for the two.

Frustration bubbled up, and Jai confronted Kavi about their waning commitment. Kavi's silence was answer enough. Resolute and determined, Jai left Mohendrapur – the city that had held them captive for too long.

As the city's grand towers and terracotta roofs faded into the distance, so did the memories of that intoxicating evening. The quest for the Moksha Vriksha, momentarily obscured by allure, now stood at the forefront of Jai's consciousness, its significance burning brightly in the light of day.

The stark shift from the vibrant city streets, teeming with age-old tales and countless distractions, to the boundless, untrodden expanse of the desert was undeniable.

Jai paused, allowing the gravity of the moment to envelop them. The city, with its many temptations, lay in the past. No longer bound to the advice of strangers; the way forward was dictated by intuition and the heart's call. With renewed vigor, Jai ventured forth, immersing themselves in the desert's solitude and the relentless search for the Moksha Vriksha.

32

PART ONE – CHAPTER SEVEN

Scorched by the Sun, Cleansed by Wisdom

The relentless sun bore down on Jai, making each step feel like an eternity. The vast desert stretched endlessly, mocking their solitude. Weakened by the journey, Jai's vision blurred and their strength waned.

Their world soon dimmed to darkness as they collapsed onto the scorching sands. It is in this vulnerable state, as Jai lies unconscious under the scorching sun, that their encounter with the wise hermit will unfold.

As Jai slowly regained consciousness, their gaze met the hermit's, who had been tending to them with gentle care. The hermit had created a sanctuary of sorts around Jai, transforming the desert landscape into a humble oasis. A makeshift shelter provided shade and refuge. The air was filled with the soothing scent of fragrant herbs and incense, instilling a sense of tranquility.

Jai blinked, momentarily disoriented, before finding their voice. "Thank you for your help," Jai murmured, their gratitude evident in their eyes.

The hermit, their face serene, nodded in acknowledgement. "You are welcome, weary traveler. It is my duty to offer solace and guidance to those who stumble upon this sacred place."

Sitting up slowly, Jai took in their surroundings, feeling a newfound calm wash over them. "This place... it feels different, peaceful. How did you create such a serene oasis amidst the desert?"

The hermit's eyes glistened with a captivating hint of mystery as they replied, "Resilience and ingenuity, weary traveler.'

Jai's curiosity grew, and their voice filled with wonder. "Might I know your name, wise hermit?"

The hermit's serene smile deepened, revealing a gentle warmth. "I am known as the hermit, a humble seeker of truth and a guardian of this sacred space. And you, what name shall I address you by?"

Jai hesitated for a moment, contemplating their journey and the purpose that led them here. "I am Jai," they finally replied, determination lacing their voice.

The hermit, their gaze fixed upon Jai's weary countenance, spoke with a voice suffused with empathy. "You bear a burden, my friend," they uttered, their words carrying the weight of understanding. "The journey has not been gentle to you, I see."

Jai, touched by the depth of the hermit's perception, nodded in acknowledgement. "Indeed," they replied, their voice tinged with a mixture of weariness and resilience. "The road has been treacherous."

The hermit's gaze softened; their face etched with understanding. "We are all travelers on this path of life, burdened by our own battles," they murmured, the weight of their words carried by the wind. They paused for a moment, as if reflecting on the vast tapestry of human existence.

Jai, now seated upright and captivated by the hermit's wisdom, looked into their eyes and spoke with sincerity. "I seek your guidance on this journey," they said, their voice laced with humility. "I seek the path to finding the Moksha Vriksha."

34

The hermit's gaze turned piercing as they posed a series of probing questions to Jai.

"Why did you enter the city of Mohendrapur?" The hermit asked, their voice carrying a weight of significance.

Jai's brow furrowed as they pondered the question. "I suppose it was the next city on the road. I just landed there.," they replied, their voice tinged with uncertainty.

The hermit continued, their questions probing deeper. "What direction did you choose when you left? How fast was your pace? How long was your stride? How deep was your breathing?"

Jai pondered for a moment, their brow furrowing with uncertainty. "I don't know," they admitted, their voice tinged with a touch of confusion. "I didn't think it mattered. I was simply moving forward, hoping to find the way."

The hermit leaned forward, their eyes gleaming with wisdom as they began to share a tale from the ancient annals of the Indus Valley. The words flowed from their lips, weaving a vivid tapestry of storytelling:

In the heart of the ancient Indus Valley, two sage healers journeyed through mystical lands, questing for enlightenment. Amidst their travels, they discovered a serene shelter ensconced in nature and chose it as a resting place.

Come morning, the second sage noticed the space transformed—cleaned with attention to detail. Intrigued, they turned to the first sage, questioning, "Why invest time in tidying a temporary abode?" The first sage, radiating calm wisdom, responded, "Every act, regardless of its perceived insignificance, profoundly impacts our worldview and inner state. In walking, we practice mindfulness. Each breath reminds us of life's sanctity. Cleaning, then, mirrors the purity and harmony within."

Reflecting upon this, the second sage grasped that all actions, thoughts, and intentions—whether in the outer world or within one's soul—held immense meaning. By being present and mindful, even mundane tasks could be transformative.

This enlightenment accompanied the sages throughout their voyage. Their steps became meditative, their breaths purposeful, and their acts of cleaning a tribute to the sanctity of their surroundings. Their heightened mindfulness reshaped their perspectives, revealing that every deed, minute or grand, had the power to influence their existence and inner well-being.

The hermit's voice resonated with profound conviction as they concluded their story. They gazed at Jai, their eyes brimming with wisdom and compassion. "Remember, dear Jai," they spoke with gentle insistence, "the key to enlightenment, to path to the Moksha Vriksha, lies not only in the external world but within the vast landscape of your own mind. It is your duty, your sacred responsibility, to keep your mind clear and clean."

Jai listened intently, feeling the weight of the hermit's words settling deep within their being. They realized that seeking Moksha Vriksha went beyond mere physical quests and external journeys. It required a diligent inward exploration, a continuous purification of thoughts, and a mindful engagement with the world around them.

The hermit extended a hand, offering support and guidance. "Walk with awareness, dear Jai," they continued, their voice filled with encouragement. "Embrace every step as a sacred dance. Breathe with consciousness, allowing the breath to cleanse and revitalize your spirit. Cleanse your surroundings and create an environment that nurtures serenity and clarity within."

Jai nodded; their heart filled with gratitude for the wisdom bestowed upon them. They understood that the quest for enlightenment was not an easy one, but it was a journey that demanded their utmost dedication and mindfulness. They realized that by keeping a clear and clean mind, they would be better equipped to navigate the challenges and embrace the profound revelations that awaited them on the path to Moksha Vriksha.

PART ONE - CHAPTER EIGHT

The Well of Indulgence

The sun cast a warm glow upon the serene landscape as Jai stood before a mystical well. The hermit had led them to this secluded spot, where the magic of self-discovery awaited. The air seemed alive with anticipation, carrying a hint of enchantment that made Jai's heart flutter.

Jai's task was simple: to retrieve a bucket of water from the well each day. It appeared to be an effortless endeavor, but as they reached for the rope and began to pull, the weight of the bucket proved overwhelming. No matter how much strength Jai exerted, the pail remained firmly rooted in the depths of the well.

Day after day, Jai faced the same frustrating outcome. Each attempt ended in failure, leaving them parched and disheartened. The desire for water intensified with each passing moment, fueling their determination to succeed. But the weight of the bucket proved to be an insurmountable obstacle.

Frustration grew within Jai's heart, and they contemplated the futility of their efforts. They questioned why the task seemed impossible and why their longing for water only increased with each failure. Doubts filled their mind, overshadowing their initial excitement.

One day, as Jai stood before the well, their mind weary and their body fatigued, a realization sparked within them. Instead of striving to lift the entire weight of the water in one go, what if they approached it differently? What if they allowed themselves to collect only a small amount at a time?

With newfound insight, Jai decided to modify their approach. They dipped the bucket into the well, allowing only a portion to fill before gently lifting it. To their surprise, the weight felt manageable, and they effortlessly raised the water to the surface. But instead of consuming the entire amount, Jai chose to drink only a small portion, savoring its refreshment, and nurturing the rest of the water to be shared with the Harad bush.

As Jai began to pour the remaining water onto the thirsty soil at the base of the Harad bush, something remarkable happened. The leaves that had once wilted and struggled now thrived with renewed vitality. The Harad bush grew greener, their stems strengthened, and blossoms unfurled in vibrant hues. Jai's heart swelled with a sense of awe and joy as they witnessed the transformation before their eyes.

Days turned into weeks, and with each passing day, the Harad bush flourished even more. Its branches became laden with ripe, succulent fruits, resembling small golden orbs of healing power. Jai marveled at the sight, knowing that within those fruits lay the essence of nourishment and strength.

As Jai savored the sweet and tangy Harad berries, they could feel their body growing stronger and more resilient. The nourishment provided by the berries fueled their muscles and invigorated their spirit. With each passing day, Jai's physical strength increased, and the weight of the water bucket became more manageable.

One day, overcome by a momentary lapse in judgment, Jai yielded to the allure of desire. Instead of savoring the Harad berries mindfully, they consumed them all in a frenzy of indulgence. The taste of the sweet fruit lingered on their lips, but an emptiness filled their heart as they realized their mistake.

With a heavy heart, Jai approached the well once more, the weight of their actions now reflected in the burdensome pail. As they reached for the handle, the force of gravity seemed to conspire against them. The weight of the water was overwhelming, pulling Jai off balance and into the depths of the well.

The air rushed past Jai's ears as they descended, their mind filled with regret and a profound sense of loss. In the darkness of the well, a realization washed over them—this was the consequence of succumbing to the insatiable cravings of desire.

The air grew thin as Jai sank deeper into the abyss, their movements becoming more frantic. Panic gripped their heart as they thrashed against the suffocating darkness. The weight of their desires bore down upon them, an inescapable burden that threatened to consume them whole.

In the depths of the well, Jai's paddle became an act of desperation, a futile attempt to stay afloat amidst the swirling currents. But with each stroke, the realization of their own folly sank deeper into their consciousness. The darkness seemed to mock their misplaced yearnings, and the water that once held promise now whispered cruel taunts.

As Jai paddled in that desolate chamber of regret, the echoes of their desires reverberated through their mind. Each stroke of the water mirrored their desperate struggle against the relentless tide of want. Yet, no matter how fiercely they fought, the well of desires seemed bottomless, their efforts in vain.

Exhaustion consumed Jai, their strength waning with each passing moment. The darkness pressed upon them, suffocating and unforgiving. In the depths of their despair, they wondered if this was to be their final resting place, forever trapped in the well of their own making.

PART ONE - CHAPTER NINE
Reflections of Regret

In the depths of the well, Jai's consciousness floated, suspended between existence and nothingness. It was as if their very essence had plunged into a realm where all light was extinguished. The void enshrouded them, an expansive abyss that stretched beyond the realms of their perception.

Within this dimension, the water hung heavy with the weight of forgotten desires, whispers of ancient mysteries echoed through the emptiness. Jai's form, now devoid of vitality, seemed to dissolve into the fabric of this mystical realm. The boundary separating the tangible from the ethereal blurred, leaving them trapped in a state of eerie suspension, neither fully present nor completely absent.

Their lifeless body drifted, vacant of any sense of direction or purpose, caught in the currents of this unfathomable void. Time lost all meaning, its steady march erased by the ceaseless expanse of darkness. Jai's physicality became a mere vessel, a conduit for the enigmatic forces that pulsed through the well.

As Jai floated in the depths of the mystical realm, their consciousness began to weave through the tapestry of their past. The waters of the well served as a mirror, reflecting images of their former self, scenes from moments they had long since let slip away.

Within the deep expanses of the well, a piece of parchment appeared, illuminated by a soft light. Elegant script danced upon its surface, each word a testament to profound emotions. Jai's fingers reached out, tracing the words they felt they had read once, long ago.

Beneath my tree, away from prying eyes,
Where whispered breezes share their gentle sighs,
I find a realm, untouched by worldly woe,
A sacred space where only dreamers go…

A vision of a tree, ancient and wise, emerged from the behind the parchment. Beneath its generous canopy, a solitary figure waited, their posture one of gentle anticipation. The rustle of leaves, the subtle fragrance of the earth, the warm gaze of the stranger — everything felt achingly familiar and sacred to Jai. They could sense a bond, a connection with this figure. Their heart recognized the figure's presence, even if their mind could not name them.

The light played through the canopy, revealing a warm glance, soft smile, and hands almost touching.

Jai's heart ached with a longing they couldn't comprehend. Memories of shared whispers, of quiet moments in the embrace of the tree, all hinting at the beginnings of a deep and profound connection.

Yet, as the emotions threatened to overflow, the defensive walls of Jai's mind rallied. "No! This... this isn't real! I've never met this person!"

The well's void shifted, painting vivid images of expansive terrains, filled with the exhilaration and the unity of seventy-one fellow scholars. Together, they journeyed, driven by the shared vision of a coiling serpent.

Within a serene clearing, the Sarvodaya Upavana unfurled, its heart holding a mystic lotus. This lotus, bathed in a celestial luminescence, seemed to whisper secrets of existence. But just as Jai was about to grasp the essence of their memory, it dissipated like mist. Jai's voice echoed with desperation, "This... this can't be real! I've never set foot there!"

From the mist, the figure of the stranger from beneath the tree materialized. Their eyes, deep pools of shared history and unfathomable love, sought Jai's gaze. As Jai looked around, they were surrounded by the familiar faces of friends and family, all cloaked in garments of celebration, their smiles warm and faces glowing with happiness. The ambiance hinted at a significant event, a union of souls.

. Joyful laughter and the soft strumming of sitars filled the air. Yet, as the overwhelming sensation of love and belonging washed over Jai, a powerful wave of denial struck. "No! This isn't real! I don't know these people!"

The well's interior shifted, weaving a scene of city streets, cold and unforgiving. Jai, as if hovering above the scene, watched a weary version of themselves, aimlessly wandering the desolate lanes. The specter below was a mirror of Jai's darkest moments: hopeless and haggard, draped in ragged clothes, eyes filled with an all-consuming despair.

Suddenly, a voice, piercing through the misty veil, pulled Jai's attention. Anaya, the seaweed alchemist, appeared. Her tear-filled eyes sought the spectral Jai with empathetic desperation.

"Jai," she beseeched, her voice quivering, ""Jai, please, we can help you heal. You don't have to go through this alone," she pleaded. But the spectral Jai, enshrouded in their self-made cocoon of misery, turned their back on her, her heartfelt entreaty fading into the ether.

Then, Kavi, the blacksmith, manifested beside Anaya. His eyes, usually firm with resolve, were clouded with sorrow. He reached out, attempting to bridge the gap between them and Jai. But, in a swift gesture, the phantom Jai drew back, leaving Kavi's outstretched hands grasping at the void. This spectral replay was a torment. The scenes laid bare Jai's past refusals, their reluctance to lean on loved ones during their most dire moments.

As the swirling depths of the well grew darker, an image began to crystallize from the shadows. It was a street, lined with towering trees. The golden glow of the setting sun painted the scene in deep oranges and purples.

In this serene setting, an older version of Jai stood, appearing more weathered but unmistakably wiser. By their side was a majestic dog, its coat a shimmering blend of ebony and gold, its eyes radiating love and compassion. This animal seemed to ground Jai, suggesting a life where they were no longer adrift.

The air around this vision hummed with promises of healing, fresh starts, and paths walked together. The ambiance, unlike previous visions, was one of hope, redemption, and a deep sense of belonging. It felt like a whisper from the future, hinting at a life filled with connection and purpose.

Yet, as the heartwarming vision started to dissolve, doubt crept into Jai's consciousness, enveloping them like a suffocating fog. The quest for the Moksha Vriksha now seemed like just another excuse to run from confronting painful truths, another avenue for escape rather than the pursuit of enlightenment. The weight of past choices and missed opportunities seemed to grow, pulling Jai's spirit further into the depths of despair.

PART ONE - CHAPTER TEN

Soaked Surrender, Sacred Scrolls

"Discipline is the key that unlocks the door to self-transformation and contentment blossoms when we embrace the present."

- Unknown

As Jai floated in the abyssal realm, surrounded by the echoes of regrets and the weight of unfulfilled dreams, a profound stillness settled upon them. It was in this stillness that Jai found themselves face to face with their own reflection, fragmented and distorted in the depths of the well.

Their mirrored self-seemed both familiar and foreign, a culmination of past choices and unexplored possibilities.

As Jai's eyes locked with their own reflection, a conversation sparked in the depths of their being. The mirrored self-gazed back with piercing intensity, and Jai sensed an accusation lingering in the silence between them. The reflection's voice echoed in Jai's mind, cutting through the dark realm.

"You have quit before," the reflection spoke, its words laced with a tinge of bitterness. "You lack discipline, always searching for the easy way out, always succumbing to doubt and fear."

Jai felt the weight of those words press upon their chest, stirring a mixture of defensiveness and self-doubt. They knew the reflection spoke an uncomfortable truth, shining a light on moments when they had turned away from challenges, abandoned dreams, or retreated from the path of perseverance.

"But what about the dreams I've pursued?" Jai's voice echoed within; their own retort laced with a determination to defend their choices. "I've ventured into the unknown, faced hardships, and embraced the uncertainty. Isn't that proof of my commitment?"

The reflection's eyes bore into Jai's, unyielding and unwavering. "Yes, you've taken steps, but how many times have you faltered? How many times have you let your doubts guide you away from your true path? You have given up on dreams that required patience, perseverance, and unwavering dedication."

Jai's heart sank under the weight of the accusation. They knew their reflection spoke of moments when fear had gripped them, when the allure of an easier path had tempted them to abandon the pursuit of their deepest desires.

Amidst the relentless accusations, a flicker of realization sparked within Jai's core. They mustered the strength to speak their truth, countering their reflection's harsh words with a newfound understanding.

"Yes, I have quit certain paths," Jai declared, their voice unwavering. "But perhaps it was not a lack of discipline, but rather the discipline to follow my heart. Each time I let go, it was a conscious decision to prioritize my inner calling, to listen to the whispers of my soul. It took discipline to trust my intuition and have the courage to explore uncharted territories."

Their reflection sneered, a mix of disbelief and skepticism etched upon its face. "You call it discipline? Quitting is the antithesis of discipline! It's an excuse, a weakness that prevents you from truly achieving greatness."

Jai's resolve solidified as they leaned forward, meeting their reflection's challenging gaze. "But isn't it a form of discipline to recognize when a path no longer aligns with our deepest values? To have the strength to let go of what no longer serves us, even when it's difficult? It takes discipline to reevaluate our choices, to pivot when necessary, and to have the courage to forge a new path."

The reflection's expression wavered, uncertainty flickering in its eyes. Jai pressed on, their voice steady and filled with conviction. "Discipline isn't solely about doggedly persisting in one direction; it's also about having the wisdom to discern when a different path beckons. It's about embracing change and growth, even if it means leaving behind what is comfortable or familiar."

The reflection's eyes, previously filled with skepticism, now softened with a hint of curiosity. "What is it that you consider so comfortable and familiar?" it inquired, almost tauntingly.

A rush of images bombarded Jai's mind: the searing glow of a raging fire, the choking scent of smoke, a sense of profound loss and grief. They glimpsed fleeting images of a love that felt both distant and familiar. Each vision seemed to pull them deeper into a labyrinth of suppressed memories, offering glimpses but never revealing the full story.

Jai's heart raced, their breaths became shallow, and the weight of those fragmented recollections threatened to pull them under. They tried to grasp the specifics, but the images slipped away like smoke through their fingers. The only constant was an overwhelming sense of pain and a desperate yearning to understand the source of these memories.

Distraught, Jai felt their heart constricting, their breathing labored. It felt as though they were reliving the trauma without truly understanding its origin or context. Just as quickly as they had emerged, the images began to fade, leaving Jai reeling and disoriented.

Their reflection, sneering once more, seemed to revel in Jai's inner turmoil. "Like water clouded by silt, your memories are tainted by the weight of your guilt," it remarked with biting scorn.

As the intensity of their debate reached its peak, the realm within the well erupted into a tumultuous battle. Jai's reflection, now consumed by anger and defiance, clashed with Jai in a fierce struggle. Their actions echoed through the watery abyss, each movement charged with determination and a stubborn refusal to yield.

Water churned and spun violently, forming a swirling vortex of chaos. The currents lashed out, spraying droplets in every direction, as if the well itself had become a tempestuous battleground. The clash between the two versions of Jai unleashed a raw power that seemed to transcend the boundaries of their existence.

Amidst the chaotic maelstrom, Jai fought with every ounce of strength they could muster. Their limbs intertwined with their reflection's, each grappling for dominance. The struggle became a dance of opposing forces, a relentless pursuit of victory over the other.

As the battle raged on, the water's force intensified, its tumultuous energy threatening to consume them both. In a final, desperate surge, the spiraling water erupted from the well, propelling Jai's reflections skyward while leaving a version of Jai gasping for air on the solid ground.

As Jai lay on the wet ground, drenched and gasping, their heart raced with a mix of exhilaration and exhaustion. The battle within the well had taken a toll, both physically and emotionally. They stared at the retreating water, their mind still reeling from the intensity of the confrontation.

A sense of bittersweet victory washed over them. They had emerged from the depths of the well, victorious in a battle against their own reflection, yet they couldn't help but feel the weight of what had been lost in the process. The confrontation had brought to the surface the deep-seated conflicts and regrets they had been carrying within.

As Jai lay on the earth, their body still recovering from the arduous battle, a sense of humility washed over them. In that vulnerable state, gasping for air and covered in the remnants of the well's waters, they realized the limits of their own strength and the futility of resisting the currents of life.

In the midst of their exhaustion, Jai turned their gaze upward, the vast expanse of the sky stretching before them. The twinkling stars above seemed to hold the answers they sought, a reminder of a higher power that transcended their individual struggles.

With each breath, Jai felt a surrender taking hold within their being. They recognized that their journey was not solely about conquering their inner demons or attaining personal achievements. It was about relinquishing control and placing their trust in something greater, something beyond their own understanding.

In that act of surrender, Jai felt a profound connection to the vastness of existence, to the intricate tapestry of life unfolding around them. They realized that the well and its mystical realm had served as a catalyst for their inner transformation, leading them to this moment of surrender and acceptance.

Lying there, gazing up at the infinite sky, Jai found solace in the realization that they were a part of something greater, a divine plan that transcended their individual desires and ambitions. They understood that surrendering to this higher power was not an act of weakness, but an act of profound strength and trust.

With a renewed sense of purpose, Jai rose from the ground, their movements guided by a newfound determination. They carried with them the echoes of their inner battles, the lessons learned, and the understanding that true liberation lay in surrendering to the flow of life, to the wisdom of the universe.

The moon cast a dim light on the path as Jai gained distance from the well. The darkness clung to them like a lingering shadow, but in the distance, a faint glow beckoned. It emanated from the humble dwelling of the hermit, nestled amidst the trees.

Jai's weary feet carried them closer to the radiant glow, their heart pulsating with a blend of anticipation and profound gratitude. The serenity and solace that emanated from the hermit's dwelling seemed to embrace them, guiding their steps as if drawing them to the haven. With each footfall, Jai's weariness transformed into a renewed sense of purpose.

As they approached the entrance, the hermit, a figure enveloped in an aura of profound wisdom and tranquility, emerged to greet Jai with a knowing smile. The lines etched upon the hermit's face spoke of countless journeys traversed, both in the outer world and within.

The hermit's gaze met Jai's, filled with curiosity and gentle concern. "Tell me, dear Jai, how was your journey through the depths of the well?"

Jai took a deep breath, their voice filled with a mixture of vulnerability and awe. "The well, dear friend, was both painful and incredible. It was a descent into the depths of my own being, a confrontation with my past regrets and desires. In its darkness, I faced the shadows that haunted me, the moments where I faltered and quit. But amidst the pain, there was also a profound sense of transformation and self-discovery."

The hermit nodded, their eyes reflecting understanding. "Pain and transformation often walk hand in hand, dear Jai. It is through facing our shadows and confronting our past that we find the strength to grow."

As they entered the hermit's dwelling, a gentle calm washed over Jai. The space exuded an aura of tranquility and reverence, adorned with symbols of wisdom and adorned tapestries that whispered stories of ancient seekers. In the center of the room, a wooden table stood, bearing a weathered manuscript that beckoned to Jai's curious gaze.

Its aged parchment seemed to hold the weight of centuries, a testament to wisdom passed down through generations. Unable to contain their inquisitiveness, Jai gestured toward the ancient tome and asked, "May I inquire about this text you hold? Its essence exudes profound significance."

The hermit's smile deepened, recognizing Jai's yearning for knowledge. "These, dear Jai, are the sacred verses of our ancestors, an ancient tapestry of wisdom passed down through generations. They are a testament to the profound seekers who have paved the way for our spiritual understanding."

Jai approached the table, their fingers gently grazing the delicate pages of the manuscripts. The hermit continued, "Within these revered texts, we find insights into the nature of existence, the interconnectedness of all beings, and the eternal quest for self-realization. They hold the timeless wisdom that has guided the spiritual leaders and enlightened souls who came before us."

As Jai reverently touched the fragile pages, a sense of awe and reverence washed over them. The weight of the words inscribed within the ancient manuscripts seemed to seep into their very being, kindling a flame of curiosity and spiritual longing. Jai looked up at the hermit, their eyes filled with a mix of wonder and anticipation.

"In these sacred verses," the hermit continued, "we discover profound insights into the essence of our existence, the intricate web of life that connects all beings, and the eternal quest for self-realization. They hold the eternal flame of wisdom that has guided the footsteps of countless seekers and illuminated the path to enlightenment."

Jai's heart swelled with a deep sense of gratitude for the hermit's guidance and the generations of spiritual leaders who had contributed to this wellspring of wisdom. Yet, a flicker of curiosity sparked within them, and they asked, "But is this all? Are we confined to the knowledge passed down from the past? Is there not something more, something yet to be revealed?"

The hermit's eyes gleamed with understanding, and their voice carried a subtle undertone of anticipation. "Indeed, dear Jai, the journey of spiritual evolution unfolds endlessly. Just as the ancient sages and enlightened souls of bygone eras unveiled timeless truths, so too does each new generation contribute to the rich tapestry of knowledge. Our sacred endeavor is to weave together the threads of fresh insights, revelations, and inquiries, adding to the ever-growing fabric of understanding."

Jai's heart quickened with anticipation as the hermit's words resonated deeply within them. The realization that their own path was intricately intertwined with the lineage of spiritual seekers throughout history sparked a profound sense of purpose. Leaning closer, they hungrily absorbed the wisdom flowing from the hermit's lips.

"In truth, the path has been etched for centuries," the hermit affirmed, their voice both gentle and resolute. "Countless seekers have trodden upon the hallowed ground you now stand upon. They, too, embarked on a quest to unravel the enigmatic mysteries of existence, seeking liberation from the ceaseless cycles of suffering and yearning for the ultimate truth."

Jai's eyes widened, their mind grappling with the weight of the hermit's words. It was as though an invisible thread, intricately woven through time, connected the footsteps of all who had traversed the path.

The hermit's voice carried the resonance of ancient wisdom as they continued to impart their knowledge. "However, dear Jai, bear this in mind: while the path has been inscribed, it is your unique journey, your individual steps, that give it life. As you traverse the path, it reveals itself, responding to the yearnings of your heart and the intentions you hold. The pursuit of the Moksha Vriksha, your current quest, is but one exquisite thread within the expansive tapestry of spiritual growth."

Jai's eyes widened with anticipation as they leaned in closer to the hermit. "But how can I find the path to the Moksha Vriksha?" they asked, their voice filled with a blend of eagerness and curiosity.

The hermit's serene expression held a profound understanding. They gently placed a hand on Jai's shoulder, conveying both reassurance and guidance. "To embark on the journey towards the Moksha Vriksha, dear Jai, you must first take the path that leads to the Refuge of Inner Stillness."

Jai's heart quickened with excitement as they listened intently to the hermit's words. The hermit continued, their voice carrying the weight of ancient wisdom. "Travel eastward, following the winding path through the ancient forest. As the sun rises, it will cast a golden glow upon the path, illuminating your way. Seek the sacred river that flows nearby, its waters murmuring ancient hymns of wisdom."

Jai nodded, absorbing each instruction with utmost reverence. The hermit's voice resonated with a sense of purpose as they continued, "As you approach the Refuge of Inner Stillness, you will notice a magnificent banyan tree, its branches stretching towards the heavens. Rest beneath its shade and await the arrival of the sages. They will provide you with the final directions that will guide you to the Moksha Vriksha."

A sense of awe and gratitude filled Jai's heart as they thanked the hermit for their invaluable guidance. With a newfound determination, Jai set forth on their journey, embracing the significance of the path that lay before them. Each step would lead them closer to the Refuge of Inner Stillness, where the next chapter of their quest awaited.

PART ONE - EPILOGUE

Teetering at the Precipice

Jai stood on the edge of a cliff, overlooking the vast expanse before them. The river, as the hermit had mentioned, flowed serenely at the bottom. The frustration within Jai simmered, for the hermit had neglected to reveal the way down to the river, leaving Jai to search in vain for a path amidst the rugged terrain.

Day had turned into night as Jai tirelessly scoured the surroundings, seeking a route to the river's embrace. Yet, each attempt seemed futile, as the cliff's steep walls and treacherous edges denied access to the elusive waters below. Weariness settled upon Jai's shoulders, mingling with a growing discontentment at the hermit's omission.

In the depths of despair, Jai teetered on the edge, feeling broken, lost, and burdened by inadequacy. The weight of their struggles threatened to plunge them into darkness. The idea of self-harm whispered momentarily, but two memories pierced through the gloom, offering glimmers of hope.

First, the image of Daya, the brave clownfish approaching the sea anemone with empathy, emerged. It reminded Jai of the power of compassion to break the cycle of violence.

The second memory was the day Jai forgave the boys who had stolen their belongings. In that act of forgiveness, Jai underwent a profound transformation, realizing that harboring anger and seeking revenge only perpetuated harm. Embracing empathy, they discovered that the path of nonviolence led to their individual path.

These memories intertwined, flooding Jai's consciousness with newfound strength. They recognized that self-inflicted harm would only deepen their wounds and impede their progress.

Jai stood on the cliff's edge, torn by desperate thoughts. Temptation beckoned them to return to the hermit's abode and steal the sacred scrolls, believing they held the key to their ultimate truth. But a memory surfaced—the baker and the bread, a lesson of non-stealing.

Jai had carved "Moksha Vriksha" upon the butter tray they gifted to the baker. Recognizing the words, the baker spoke of the tree, providing an unexpected guide on Jai's journey. This profound connection ignited a renewed determination within Jai. They understood that choosing the path of integrity, as they did by refraining from stealing the bread, would lead to rewards and insights that could aid them in uncovering their ultimate truth.

As Jai stood on the cliff's edge, frustration and resentment surged within. They blamed others for their misfortunes—the boys, the baker, the blacksmith, the seaweed alchemist, even the hermit.

Jai felt a surge of anger and injustice, as if the world conspired against them. However, amidst this sea of discontent, a memory resurfaced, piercing through the veil of victimhood. It was a memory of the blacksmith, Kavi, acknowledging Jai's role in the theft of their belongings.

Kavi had reminded them that it was their own choice to leave the shelter, knowing the pervasive injustices that plagued the city. In that moment, Jai had accepted responsibility for their actions, acknowledging the role they played in bringing themselves to this point of being trapped on the cliff.

Jai, teetering on the edge of the cliff, found their mind drifting back to the intoxicating night spent with Kavi, the blacksmith. The memories of that evening flooded their thoughts, luring them with the allure of indulgence and fleeting pleasures. For a moment, Jai wished they had stayed, succumbing to the seductive charms of those mysterious creatures and the numbing effects of the potion.

Regret gnawed at Jai's conscience as they contemplated the path not taken. They yearned for the reckless abandon, the temporary escape from reality that such nights provided. But then, in the depths of their recollection, another aspect of Kavi's story emerged—the struggle with indulgence.

Jai remembered the grip of addiction that held Kavi tightly within the confines of the city. Kavi's pursuit of immediate gratification had overshadowed their search for the Moksha Vriksha, binding them to a life of transient pleasures and momentary highs. The practice of celibacy and fidelity, the commitment to a higher purpose, had eluded Kavi, consumed by the allure of substances and fleeting encounters.

In this realization, a new understanding washed over Jai's consciousness. They recognized the stark contrast between themselves and Kavi. They possessed a strength that transcended the allure of temporary pleasures and the shackles of addiction. Jai yearned for a deeper connection, a profound transformation that went beyond the surface-level indulgences of that intoxicating night.

Jai's mind swirled with a maelstrom of thoughts, a chaotic whirlwind that threatened to consume their clarity. It was as if the clutter of their internal world had manifested itself in a tumultuous storm within their mind. But amid the chaos, a glimmer of clarity emerged.

Like a beacon of light cutting through the fog, Jai's memory conjured the tale of the two sages shared by the hermit. The story spoke of the profound connection between external and internal cleanliness, highlighting the significance of every action in shaping one's reality.

Jai's mind, once cluttered and fragmented, began to find solace in this revelation. They realized that every task, no matter how seemingly insignificant, had the potential to shape their internal landscape. It was the thoughts and intentions woven into their actions that held the power to create their lived experience.

In this moment of newfound clarity, Jai took a step back from the edge of the cliff. They surveyed the forest floor near the precipice, cluttered with debris and fallen leaves. With a renewed sense of purpose, Jai embarked on a mission to create cleanliness amidst the chaos.

Each deliberate movement, each act of cleaning, became a symbolic gesture of tending to the internal world. As Jai cleared the forest floor, a serene tranquility settled within them. The very act of cleaning became a meditative practice, a way to cultivate inner clarity amidst the external disarray.

Unbeknownst to anyone else, hidden within Jai's meticulous cleaning, lay a purpose beyond mere tidiness. Jai was preparing a pristine runway, a clean path that would serve as a springboard for their leap of faith from the edge of the cliff. But for now, that intention remained veiled, known only to Jai's resolute heart.

In the cleansed forest, Jai's proud gaze swept over their accomplishment—a testament to their efforts. Their mind drifted to a significant realization at the well, where balance and moderation revealed themselves.

Struggling with the weight of a full bucket, Jai discovered that their strength alone couldn't conquer it. But in that realization, they found a simple solution—wanting less. By filling the bucket partially, they could manage its weight and move forward.

Jai's understanding extended beyond themselves. They shared the excess water with a thirsty bush, which flourished and bore fruit. This act of selflessness nourished Jai too, making them stronger.

Yet, a cautionary tale followed their growth. A day of over-indulgence led to disregarding balance and attempting to lift a full bucket, only to be pulled into the depths of the well.

This memory served as a reminder of the risks of over-indulgence and the importance of maintaining equilibrium. Jai learned the lesson, recognizing the consequences of unrestrained self-gratification.

As Jai took a few steps away from the cliff's edge, their mind ventured back to the depths of the well—a place where they had encountered a past versions of themselves, burdened by the weights of silent struggles. In that haunting encounter, Jai had come face to face with the profound depth of their own pain and sorrow.

It had been a heart-wrenching experience, descending into the darkness and confronting the inner demons that had plagued them for far too long. But amidst the despair, Jai discovered a revelation—a connection to a deeper, more resilient aspect of themselves. In the depths of the well, they had tapped into an inner reservoir of strength.

From that encounter, Jai gleaned an invaluable lesson—the importance of discipline in its myriad forms. It wasn't just about adhering to strict rules or routines; it encompassed the discipline to let go of what no longer served them, the courage to face their shadows, and the determination to emerge stronger on the other side.

The moonlight cast a serene glow over the forest floor, making the carefully cleaned runway shimmer. The wind caressed Jai's cheeks, their heart pulsing with eager anticipation.

Memories of past struggles and lessons surfaced: the power of compassion, the essence of non-stealing, accepting responsibility, the perils of overindulgence, the depth of discipline, and the balance of life. Each lesson formed a thread, weaving a tapestry of understanding.

As Jai took a deep breath, preparing for the leap, a unique sight caught their attention. Despite the night, a lone butterfly danced in the moonlight, its wings reflecting the soft glow. This nocturnal butterfly, defying the norms of its kind, seemed to beckon Jai forward, embodying the beauty of surrender and the magic of trust in the unknown.

Taking this as a sign, Jai remembered the moments in the well, where surrender had become a transformative power. With the butterfly's graceful flight as inspiration, they sprinted, feeling the weight of the lessons they carried, and launched themselves off the cliff.

The leap was not of despair but of faith; faith in the journey, in the lessons learned, and in the mysteries of the universe yet to be unveiled. As Jai soared, the world around felt both real and dreamlike. The distant silhouette of the Moksha Vriksha, bathed in moonlight, stood as a testament to the path ahead.

Jai, in this suspended moment between the past and the future, felt an overwhelming connection to everything—the moon, the stars, the nocturnal butterfly, and the very essence of life itself.

Part 2

The Refuge
of Inner Stillness

PART TWO - PROLOGUE
The Descent

The wind howled in Jai's ears as they hurtled through the air, their body plummeting towards the ground below. The world around them became a blur of swirling colors and shapes, a kaleidoscope of sensations that blurred the line between reality and dream. Jai's heart raced in their chest, a mixture of fear and exhilaration pulsating through their veins.

With each passing second, the fall seemed to stretch into eternity. Jai's eyes darted frantically, searching for any familiar landmark or sign of guidance. In the distance, a glimmer of hope emerged—a distant silhouette of the Moksha Vriksha, its magnificent presence filling Jai's vision. It radiated a mystical allure, further igniting the fire of determination within Jai's heart.

As Jai continued their descent, the world below transformed into a tapestry of wonders. Jagged cliffs, lush forests, and meandering rivers flashed by in fleeting moments. Jai's senses heightened, their body attuned to the rush of the wind and the sheer exhilaration of the fall. It was a dance with destiny, an epic crossing of a threshold.

Amidst the chaos of the descent, a profound stillness settled within Jai. The world around them seemed to fade away, leaving only the sound of their own breath and the beating of their heart. Time became elastic, stretching and distorting as Jai surrendered to the embrace of the freefall.

In that suspended moment, a sense of clarity emerged, an unwavering focus that transcended the physical realm.

And then, with a jarring collision that shook their very core, the weight of existence came crashing back upon Jai. The air filled with the sound of snapping branches, their jagged edges tearing through the space around them. Each collision with a tree branch intensified the pain, amplifying the echoes of anguish within Jai's being. Their body twisted and contorted, helpless against the forces of gravity and the unforgiving obstacles in their path.

Agony engulfed them, overwhelming their senses and shrouding their awareness. Yet, even in the midst of this torment, a flicker of resilience burned within Jai's spirit. They refused to succumb to the overwhelming pain, drawing upon an inner reserve of strength and determination. Through gritted teeth and with every ounce of willpower, they summoned the energy to endure.

And then, with a bone-shattering impact, reality crashed back into Jai. Pain reverberated through every fiber of their being as their body collided with the unforgiving ground below. Torment consumed them, enveloping their senses and stealing their consciousness.

PART TWO - CHAPTER ONE

The Reintegration Awakening

"The body is a sacred temple, and through mindful movement, we connect the physical and the spiritual, finding balance and harmony within."

— Unknown

When Jai finally awoke, the world had changed. The sun had risen, painting the sky with hues of gold and casting a warm, radiant glow over the transformed landscape. Jai's eyes fluttered open, and they found themselves lying under the protective shade of a magnificent banyan tree, its sprawling branches reaching towards the heavens with a sense of ancient wisdom. The air was laden with stillness, as if the entire universe held its breath in anticipation of Jai's arrival.

Jai's weary body succumbed to exhaustion once more, and they drifted into a deep slumber under the banyan tree's nurturing embrace. Time slipped away as dreams weaved through their consciousness, carrying whispers of forgotten truths and untapped potentials.

When Jai's eyes opened again, a glimmer of anticipation danced within their gaze. Figures emerged from the horizon, their silhouettes gradually taking shape.

As the figures approached Jai, their caring presence enveloped them. Jai's body, ravaged by serious injuries, rendered them unable to walk. The figures revealed themselves as sages, emanating an aura of wisdom and compassion. With gentle concern, they inquired about Jai's name and how Jai had arrived at this place. Jai shared that it was the hermit who had guided them here.

The sages welcomed Jai with open hearts, acknowledging the significance of their encounter. They explained that the magnificent banyan tree under which they stood served as a "solitude space" where the sages could momentarily break their sacred vow of silence known as Mauna. Outside the confines of this tree, however, their commitment to silence would be steadfast and unwavering.

Understanding the sacredness of their vow, Jai felt a profound sense of privilege to be in the presence of these silent masters. Overwhelmed by exhaustion, Jai succumbed to sleep once again, trusting in the care and support of the sages who gently carried him on a stretcher they had crafted from the surrounding forest.

As Jai awoke, they found themselves in the peaceful Refuge of Inner Stillness, surrounded by the silent presence of the sages who continued to observe their sacred vow of Mauna. Jai lay comfortably, sipping a warm cup of tea, as their gaze rested upon the sages engaged in a mesmerizing display of synchronized movement.

In graceful harmony, the sages contorted their bodies with fluid precision. Each motion seemed to emanate a profound sense of harmony and balance. As Jai observed this silent dance, they could sense the intention and mindfulness behind each movement.

As one of the sages settled beside Jai, a tranquil aura enveloped them both. The sage, committed to observing Mauna, remained silent but conveyed their wisdom through subtle gestures and gentle movements. Sitting alongside Jai, they embarked on a graceful sequence of motions, inviting Jai to follow their lead

The sage began by assuming a seated position, drawing their knees toward their chest and extending their arms gracefully toward the sky. With a deliberate tilt at the hips, they reached toward their toes, and Jai instinctively mirrored their actions. The rhythmic flow of their synchronized movements fostered a sense of connection and harmony.

Continuing the gentle exploration, the sage introduced twists, guiding their torso in gentle rotations from side to side. Jai watched closely, mirroring the sage's movements with attentiveness and receptiveness. The sage's body seemed to move with effortless grace, and Jai sought to embody that same fluidity, following their lead.

Under the sage's patient guidance, Jai followed their lead and settled into various positions, each held with intention and purpose. The sage's experienced hands gently adjusted Jai's posture, ensuring comfort and alignment.

As Jai lay on the ground, the sage rolled a soft blanket and carefully placed it beneath Jai's lower back, providing gentle support and encouraging a sense of release and relaxation. The blanket created a subtle elevation, allowing Jai's spine to find a curve and relieve some tension held in the lower back.

With mindful precision, the sage skillfully stacked blankets, creating a bolster-like support for Jai's legs. By elevating the legs, this arrangement offered a nurturing release for tired muscles, promoting circulation and rejuvenation. Jai's legs rested upon the blanket stack, finding a position of comfort and stability.

As time went by, Jai delved deeper into the gentle yoga guided by the silent sage. With each passing day, Jai's body grew stronger and more flexible, allowing them to sink into the poses with greater ease. The once-challenging postures gradually became familiar territory, as Jai's muscles responded to the gentle movements.

As Jai recovered from their injuries, they found solace in the rhythmic flow of the practice. Each pose became an opportunity for healing and self-discovery. Jai embraced the quiet moments of reflection, feeling the subtle energy coursing through their body as they moved from one posture to another.

The yoga practice became a gateway to inner stillness and resilience. Jai's breath synchronized with the movements, bringing a sense of peace and clarity. With every stretch and twist, Jai shed layers of physical and emotional tension, finding balance and harmony within.

Over time, Jai not only benefited from the sage's care but also became an active participant in the daily activities of the refuge. They assisted with cleaning, cooking, and tending to the needs of the sages. The simple acts of service and mindfulness further deepened their connection to the practice, as they discovered the joy of selfless giving and the unity of shared responsibilities.

In this montage of time, Jai's transformation unfolded. From a state of injury and vulnerability, they emerged as a beacon of resilience and gratitude. Jai's journey of recovery became intertwined with their spiritual awakening, finding solace, growth, and healing in the presence of the silent sages.

PART TWO –
CHAPTER TWO

The Breath's Embrace

"Conscious breath, life's gentle art,
Unites body, soul, every part.
In stillness found, a calm divine,
Interconnected, we align."

- Unknown

The Sages moved in unison, their silent footsteps echoing through the serene forest as they guided Jai along the winding path. The gentle murmur of the river accompanied their journey, a soothing melody that seemed to hold the secrets of the land.

As they approached the majestic Banyan tree, its sprawling branches extended like an open embrace, welcoming them to the sanctuary of whispers. Here, the Sages would momentarily break their vow of silence, allowing their voices to intertwine in a harmonious exchange.

Jai felt a sense of anticipation and reverence as they entered the sanctuary. The air was filled with an aura of sacredness, as if the very atmosphere held the weight of the Sages' collective wisdom. In this hallowed space, the veils between silence and speech, between introspection and expression, seemed to thin.

The Sages gathered around the ancient tree; their eyes filled with a quiet intensity. Jai watched with a mix of curiosity and reverence, knowing that within this sacred pause, profound insights awaited.

With great care and intention, the Sages settled into a circle, their faces radiant with a deep knowing. As they sat in stillness, a gentle breeze whispered through the leaves, as if nature itself held its breath in anticipation of the exchange to come.

"You've recovered from your fall quite well, I see," spoke one of the Sages, their voice carrying a tone of warmth and reassurance.

Jai, grateful for their concern, responded, "Yes, thanks to your care and guidance, I have regained my strength and mobility."

Another Sage, their voice gentle like a soothing melody, inquired, "How are you feeling now, Jai? How has your journey of healing and self-discovery unfolded?"

Jai paused for a moment, reflecting on their experiences, before sharing, "I feel a newfound sense of vitality and purpose. Through the practice of yoga and your teachings, I have learned not only to walk again but also to truly live and embrace the fullness of life."

A third Sage, their eyes filled with wisdom, nodded and spoke softly, "And now, Jai, you express a desire to delve deeper into the practice of yoga, to explore the intricate art of bending and contorting the body. You wish to learn to stand on your forearms and head."

Jai's eyes sparkled with determination as they replied, "Indeed, I want to learn the physical prowess of these advanced poses, but I also understand that there is more to them than meets the eye. I want to cultivate the strength, flexibility, and stillness necessary to achieve them."

A fourth Sage smiled and responded, "My dear Jai, you have captured the essence of the ancient practice of yoga. These physical postures, or asanas, are not merely about achieving impressive feats. They are tools to teach us how to sit, how to find steadiness and comfort in stillness."

With profound insight, the first Sage continued, "Yoga is a practice that encompasses not only the physical body but also the mind, breath, and spirit. Through dedicated practice, we cultivate balance, harmony, and self-awareness. The ultimate goal is to prepare the body and mind for meditation, to enter a state of deep inner stillness and connection."

Jai listened attentively, their heart resonating with the wisdom shared by the Sage. They realized that the path of yoga was not solely about physical accomplishments but a journey of self-discovery, self-mastery, and inner peace.

As the Sages encircled Jai, the air seemed to shimmer with a sense of anticipation. Sage One, their eyes filled with gentle wisdom, turned their attention to Jai and softly spoke, "Take a breath, dear Jai. Inhale deeply, and exhale fully."

Jai followed the Sage's guidance, feeling the air fill their lungs. As they released their breath, a cascade of tension dissolved into the atmosphere. It was a simple act, yet profound in its transformative power.

Sage One's voice carried a hint of playfulness as they continued, "You see, Jai, the breath is a remarkable teacher. It effortlessly dances between the realms of conscious and unconscious, guiding us on a journey of awareness and self-discovery."

Intrigued, Jai leaned closer, eager to delve deeper into the mysteries of breath. Sage Two, with a serene smile, joined the conversation. "Just as the waves of the ocean rise and fall, our breaths the rhythm of existence.

It reminds us that we are intimately connected to the ebb and flow of the universe."

Sage Three, their voice carrying a gentle yet profound tone, added to the unfolding wisdom. "And moments ago, before we asked you to take a breath, you were breathing. You didn't need to think about breathing. And yet, you breathed effortlessly." They paused, allowing the significance of their words to sink in.

As they walked in a gentle circle around the majestic Banyan tree, the tranquil sanctuary within Mauna, Jai continued their conversation with the Sages. The rhythmic sound of their footsteps on the earth created a soothing cadence, harmonizing with the timeless wisdom being shared.

Sage One, their voice carrying a soft yet commanding presence, guided Jai's awareness to the act of walking. "Place one foot in front of the other, and be mindful," they reiterated, their words grounded in deep intention.

Jai followed the instruction, their steps aligning with the sacred space of the tree. As they circled around the tree, they felt a subtle energy enveloping them.

Sage Two, walking alongside Jai, interjected with a gentle smile, "And now, you're walking." Their words seemed to echo through the air, inviting Jai to explore the layers of their own existence.

Sage Three, attuned to Jai's confusion, offered a reassuring insight, "And, moments ago, while we were chatting, you were walking. You didn't need to think about walking. And yet, you walked effortlessly."

Jai's brow furrowed, their mind grappling with the paradoxical nature of these actions. Yet, as they continued their circular path, a sense of clarity began to emerge.

Sage Four, their voice carrying the wisdom of ages, stepped in to shed light on the mystery. "Dear Jai, the dance between voluntary and non-voluntary actions is an invitation to mindfulness and meditation. Just as walking effortlessly happens to us, it can occur for us, and we can be active participants in it. It is in this dance that we find the profound union of our own agency and the natural unfolding of life."

Sage One, with deep reverence for the sacredness of the Banyan tree, nodded in agreement. "Walking, like breath, reveals the ever-present connection between our individual will and the greater flow of existence. It is through mindfulness that we come to embody this union, finding peace and presence in each step."

As Jai stood among the Sages, a sense of anticipation filled the air. Sage One, with a gentle smile, spoke first. "Jai, my dear, you have embarked on a remarkable journey healing your body. Now, it is time to explore the power of breath, for it is through conscious breathing that we connect with the very essence of life."

Sage Two nodded in agreement. "Indeed, Jai. The breath is the bridge that unites the physical body and the subtle realms of the mind and spirit. By delving into the practice of breathing techniques, you will unlock new dimensions of awareness and cultivate a profound sense of inner peace."

Sage Three, their eyes shining with wisdom, added, "Each breath we take is a gift, an opportunity to tap into the boundless energy and vitality that resides within us. Through these techniques, you will learn to harness the breath's transformative power and bring harmony to your entire being."

Sage Four, with a serene presence, concluded, "Jai, as you embrace these breathing practices, remember that they are not mere techniques to master. They are gateways to self-realization, tools to deepen your connection with the divine and the world around you. Let your breath be your guide, leading you to profound insights and awakening."

With these words, the Sages imparted the significance of the next phase in Jai's journey—to explore the realm of breath and discover the transformative potential it held. The pages that followed would be filled with descriptions and instructions for various breathing techniques, guiding Jai on a path of inner exploration and liberation.

With reverence, Jai and the Sages made their way back along the winding path, leaving the shelter of the tree behind. The gentle rustling of leaves accompanied their steps, as if nature itself whispered its blessings and guidance.

Soon, they arrived at the familiar gates of the Refuge of Inner Stillness. The sanctuary welcomed them back, enveloping them in a sense of peace and tranquility. Within these sacred grounds, they would continue their exploration of breath, diving deeper into the realms of meditation and mindfulness.

As they entered the refuge, the Sages led Jai to their quarters, a simple yet serene space where they would reside during this phase of their journey. Surrounded by the serenity of Mauna, Jai felt a renewed sense of purpose and an eagerness to embrace the teachings that awaited them.

The pages of their story turned once again, unveiling the next chapter of their adventure—a profound exploration dedicated to the practice of breath. Guided by the Sages, Jai would embark on a journey deep into the intricate world of pranayama, discovering the untapped potential of their breath and the boundless possibilities it held.

Pranayama

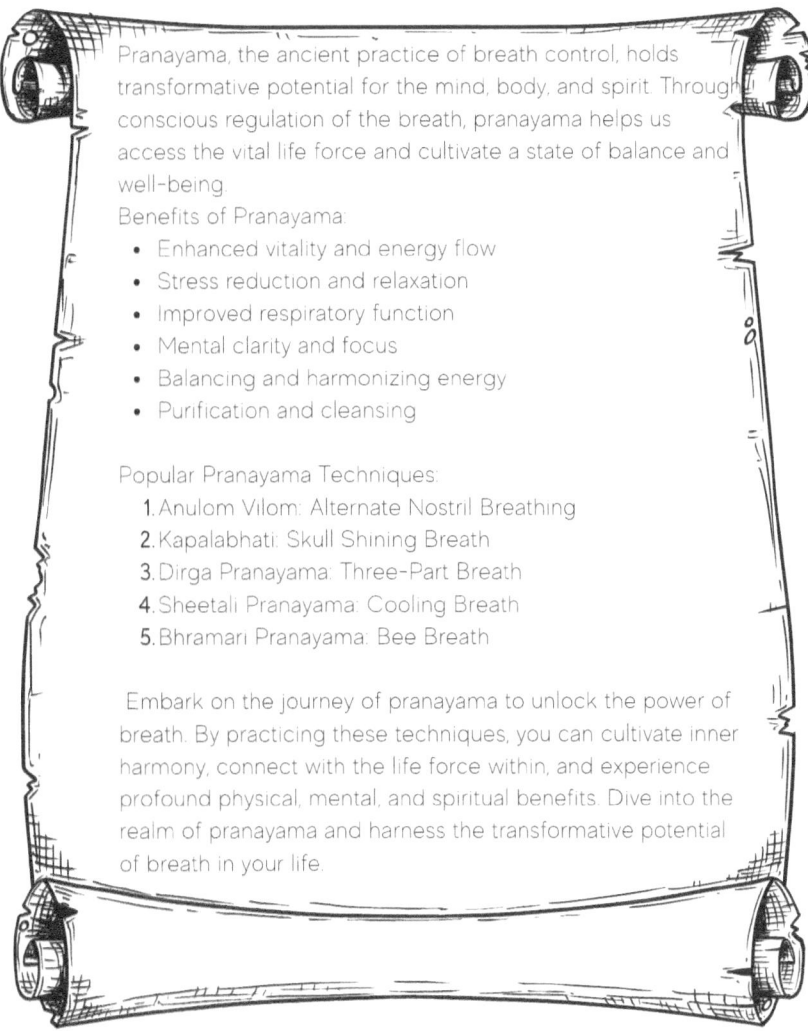

Pranayama, the ancient practice of breath control, holds transformative potential for the mind, body, and spirit. Through conscious regulation of the breath, pranayama helps us access the vital life force and cultivate a state of balance and well-being.

Benefits of Pranayama:
- Enhanced vitality and energy flow
- Stress reduction and relaxation
- Improved respiratory function
- Mental clarity and focus
- Balancing and harmonizing energy
- Purification and cleansing

Popular Pranayama Techniques:
1. Anulom Vilom: Alternate Nostril Breathing
2. Kapalabhati: Skull Shining Breath
3. Dirga Pranayama: Three-Part Breath
4. Sheetali Pranayama: Cooling Breath
5. Bhramari Pranayama: Bee Breath

Embark on the journey of pranayama to unlock the power of breath. By practicing these techniques, you can cultivate inner harmony, connect with the life force within, and experience profound physical, mental, and spiritual benefits. Dive into the realm of pranayama and harness the transformative potential of breath in your life.

Sama Vritti Pranayama

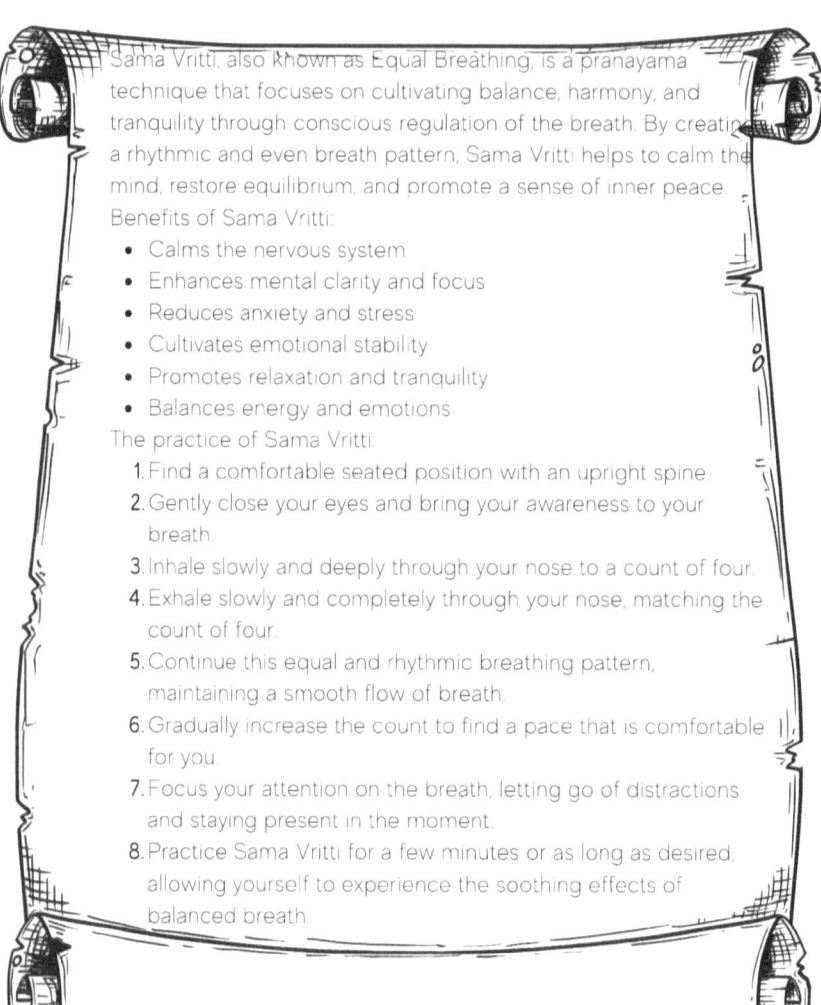

Sama Vritti, also known as Equal Breathing, is a pranayama technique that focuses on cultivating balance, harmony, and tranquility through conscious regulation of the breath. By creating a rhythmic and even breath pattern, Sama Vritti helps to calm the mind, restore equilibrium, and promote a sense of inner peace.

Benefits of Sama Vritti:

- Calms the nervous system
- Enhances mental clarity and focus
- Reduces anxiety and stress
- Cultivates emotional stability
- Promotes relaxation and tranquility
- Balances energy and emotions

The practice of Sama Vritti:

1. Find a comfortable seated position with an upright spine.
2. Gently close your eyes and bring your awareness to your breath.
3. Inhale slowly and deeply through your nose to a count of four.
4. Exhale slowly and completely through your nose, matching the count of four.
5. Continue this equal and rhythmic breathing pattern, maintaining a smooth flow of breath.
6. Gradually increase the count to find a pace that is comfortable for you.
7. Focus your attention on the breath, letting go of distractions and staying present in the moment.
8. Practice Sama Vritti for a few minutes or as long as desired, allowing yourself to experience the soothing effects of balanced breath.

Ujjayi Pranayama

Ujjayi Breath, also known as Victorious Breath or Ocean Breath, is an essential component of many yoga practices and can be particularly beneficial for building heat within the body. When incorporated into your yoga practice, Ujjayi Breath helps generate internal warmth, which can enhance the overall experience and deepen your connection to the practice.

Here's how to incorporate Ujjayi Breath to build heat in your yoga practice:

1. Begin by finding a comfortable and steady posture, such as Mountain Pose (Tadasana), at the top of your mat.
2. Close your eyes gently and take a moment to establish a steady and balanced stance. Allow your body to relax, and bring your awareness to your breath.
3. Start breathing deeply through your nose, filling your lungs completely. As you exhale, engage the muscles at the back of your throat to create a slight constriction, producing the characteristic "oceanic" sound of Ujjayi Breath.
4. Once you have established the Ujjayi Breath, synchronize it with your movements. Inhale deeply as you expand or reach, and exhale slowly as you contract or fold.
5. As you flow through your yoga practice, maintain a steady and rhythmic Ujjayi Breath. The breath should be audible to yourself, but not overly loud.

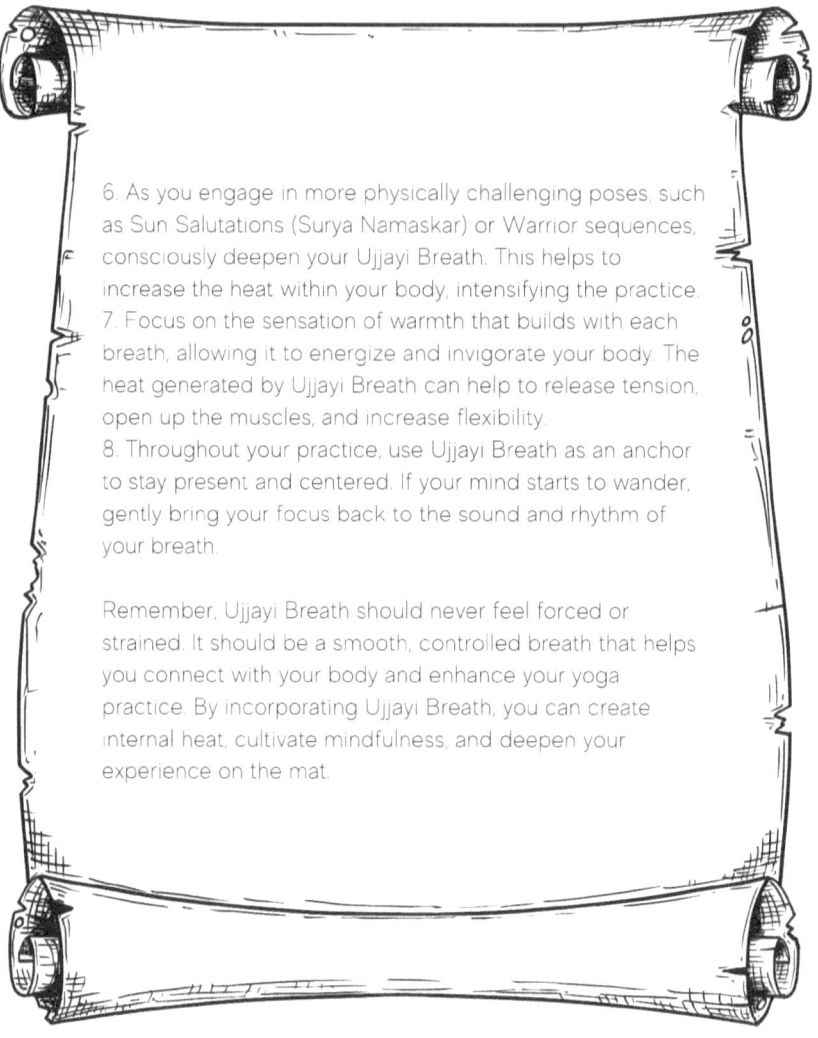

6. As you engage in more physically challenging poses, such as Sun Salutations (Surya Namaskar) or Warrior sequences, consciously deepen your Ujjayi Breath. This helps to increase the heat within your body, intensifying the practice.
7. Focus on the sensation of warmth that builds with each breath, allowing it to energize and invigorate your body. The heat generated by Ujjayi Breath can help to release tension, open up the muscles, and increase flexibility.
8. Throughout your practice, use Ujjayi Breath as an anchor to stay present and centered. If your mind starts to wander, gently bring your focus back to the sound and rhythm of your breath.

Remember, Ujjayi Breath should never feel forced or strained. It should be a smooth, controlled breath that helps you connect with your body and enhance your yoga practice. By incorporating Ujjayi Breath, you can create internal heat, cultivate mindfulness, and deepen your experience on the mat.

Dirga Pranayama

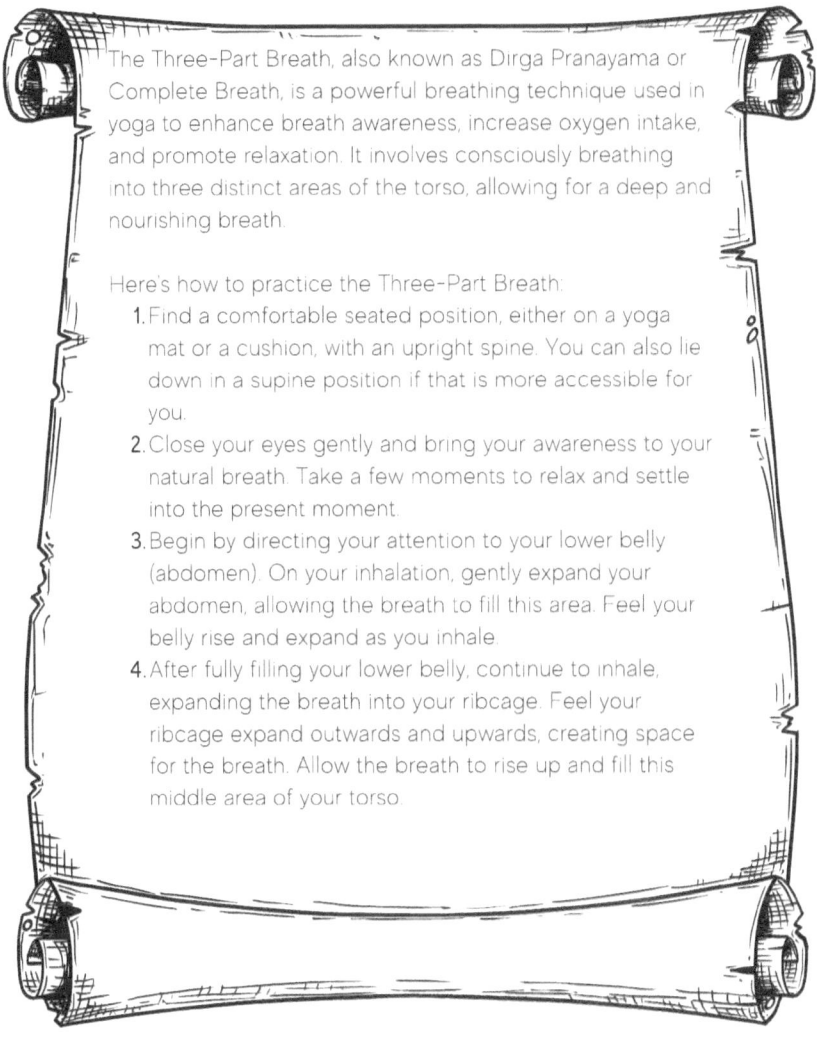

The Three-Part Breath, also known as Dirga Pranayama or Complete Breath, is a powerful breathing technique used in yoga to enhance breath awareness, increase oxygen intake, and promote relaxation. It involves consciously breathing into three distinct areas of the torso, allowing for a deep and nourishing breath.

Here's how to practice the Three-Part Breath:

1. Find a comfortable seated position, either on a yoga mat or a cushion, with an upright spine. You can also lie down in a supine position if that is more accessible for you.

2. Close your eyes gently and bring your awareness to your natural breath. Take a few moments to relax and settle into the present moment.

3. Begin by directing your attention to your lower belly (abdomen). On your inhalation, gently expand your abdomen, allowing the breath to fill this area. Feel your belly rise and expand as you inhale.

4. After fully filling your lower belly, continue to inhale, expanding the breath into your ribcage. Feel your ribcage expand outwards and upwards, creating space for the breath. Allow the breath to rise up and fill this middle area of your torso.

Dirga Pranayama
Continued

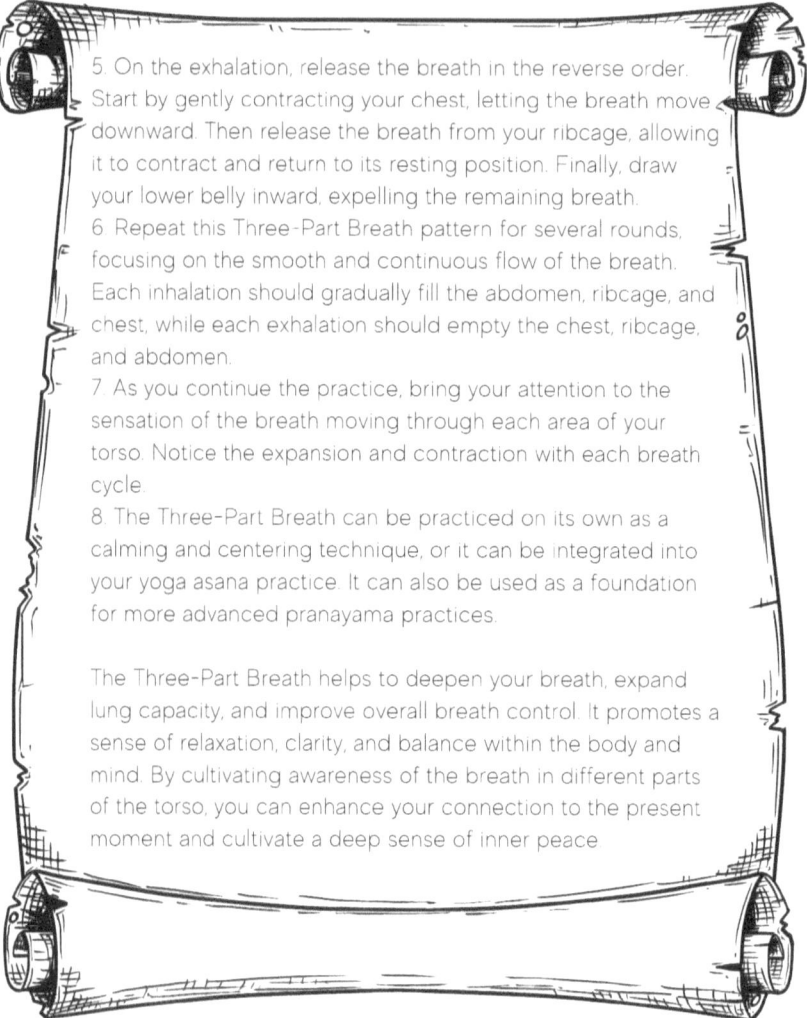

5. On the exhalation, release the breath in the reverse order. Start by gently contracting your chest, letting the breath move downward. Then release the breath from your ribcage, allowing it to contract and return to its resting position. Finally, draw your lower belly inward, expelling the remaining breath.

6. Repeat this Three-Part Breath pattern for several rounds, focusing on the smooth and continuous flow of the breath. Each inhalation should gradually fill the abdomen, ribcage, and chest, while each exhalation should empty the chest, ribcage, and abdomen.

7. As you continue the practice, bring your attention to the sensation of the breath moving through each area of your torso. Notice the expansion and contraction with each breath cycle.

8. The Three-Part Breath can be practiced on its own as a calming and centering technique, or it can be integrated into your yoga asana practice. It can also be used as a foundation for more advanced pranayama practices.

The Three-Part Breath helps to deepen your breath, expand lung capacity, and improve overall breath control. It promotes a sense of relaxation, clarity, and balance within the body and mind. By cultivating awareness of the breath in different parts of the torso, you can enhance your connection to the present moment and cultivate a deep sense of inner peace.

PART TWO-
CHAPTER THREE
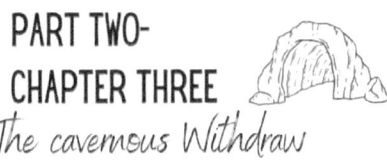
The cavernous Withdraw

"In stillness and silence, we turn inward, withdrawing from external distractions, and discover the vastness of our own inner landscape."

- Unknown

Jai sat alone in the heart of the serene forest, surrounded by the gentle whispers of nature. With closed eyes, they immersed themselves in the practice of breathing techniques, seeking to still the restless waves of their mind and find inner peace. Inhale, exhale, each breath a steady rhythm, connecting them to the vital energy coursing through their being.

As Jai delved deeper into their practice, their awareness expanded, attuning to the subtle sounds of the forest. Amidst the symphony of birdsongs and rustling leaves, a distinct sound caught their attention—the troubled breath of a deer. The soft panting was a poignant reminder of the interconnectedness of all living beings, and Jai's heart filled with compassion.

Curiosity and concern tugged at Jai's spirit, compelling them to investigate the source of the deer's distress. With gentle movements, they rose from their meditation cushion and followed the sound, traversing through the dappled shades of the forest.

Guided by the rhythmic breath of the deer, Jai navigated through the underbrush, their footsteps careful and mindful. Their own breath remained steady and grounded, serving as an anchor amidst the flurry of thoughts and emotions.

Finally, at the edge of a small clearing, Jai discovered the trapped deer, its fragile form entangled amidst the unforgiving embrace of vines and branches. The deer's panicked eyes met Jai's, and in that silent exchange, a bond formed—a recognition of shared vulnerability and the power of compassion.

Jai approached the deer with gentle steps, radiating a soothing presence. They crouched down, their breath aligning with the deer's troubled panting. In a tender act of unity, Jai began mirroring the deer's breath, exhaling softly as the deer exhaled, inhaling as the deer inhaled.

As the tranquil rhythm of synchronized breath enveloped them, a sense of calm permeated the clearing. The deer, reassured by Jai's presence and the harmonious connection of their breath, ceased its struggle against the entanglement.

With patient care, Jai untangled the vines and branches, freeing the deer from its temporary prison. The deer, its eyes now filled with gratitude, took a moment to collect itself before bounding away, a symbol of resilience and liberation.

With the radiant light of freedom still shimmering in the air, Jai's gaze was drawn to a distant sight—an enigmatic cave nestled amidst the towering ancient trees. Its entrance beckoned like a portal to hidden mysteries and profound revelations.

Curiosity kindled within Jai's heart, prompting them to embark on a journey toward the cave. Step by step, their feet carried them across the untrodden path, guided by an invisible thread of destiny. The forest whispered secrets in hushed tones, as if preparing Jai for the profound encounter that awaited them.

As Jai drew nearer, the cave's aura grew more palpable—a potent blend of mystery, stillness, and a touch of untamed wilderness. The world outside began to fade, its cacophony of noise silenced by the rhythmic beat of Jai's own breath. They sensed an invitation to delve deeper into the recesses of their being, where dormant truths awaited their awakening.

With each stride, anticipation coursed through Jai's veins, their breath steady and purposeful. The journey to the cave mirrored the journey within—an exploration of the vast landscapes of the mind, where the layers of illusions and self-discovery intertwined.

Finally, Jai reached the mouth of the cave—a threshold between the known and the unknown. Its darkness embraced them, promising both shadow and illumination. Hesitation danced on the edges of their consciousness, but an inner resolve propelled them forward.

Stepping into the embrace of the cave, Jai's senses dulled, their body enveloped by a veil of darkness. As they ventured deeper, the world outside faded away, consumed by the void that seemed to dwell within the cavernous depths.

The absence of light held a mystical power, inviting Jai to surrender their reliance on external stimuli. In this realm of shadows and silence, the boundaries between the self and the outside world blurred, and the distractions that once clamored for attention fell into a hushed stillness.

Time lost its grip within the cave's embrace, and Jai became acutely aware of the vast expanse of the present moment. The temperature of the cave became inconsequential, as if the very concept of hot or cold dissolved into the ethereal realms.

Jai's being melded with the solidity of the stone, their breath synchronizing with the cavern's ancient exhales. As they ventured deeper, a curious transformation occurred, dissolving the boundary between Jai's physical form and the cave's stony embrace. In this mystical convergence, the sensations of touch began to fade, as if the very essence of Jai's being transcended the physical realm. The tactile world slipped away, allowing awareness to merge with the timeless presence of the cave, where the boundaries of the self and the environment blurred in unity.

As Jai's eyes adjusted to the dimness, the vastness of the cave revealed its hidden treasure—a tapestry of stars scattered across the ceiling, casting a mesmerizing glow in the darkness. Familiar constellations took shape, their patterns whispering stories of ancient myths and cosmic journeys.

Intrigued and awe-struck, Jai's mind sought an explanation for this celestial spectacle. Logical reasoning interwove with the threads of curiosity, leading Jai to consider the possibility that these stars were but projections of their own mind, born within the void of the cave's embrace. A profound realization began to dawn on Jai, that in the absence of all external light, the mind, like a masterful artist, could paint its own universe of stars, bringing forth a majestic cosmos from the depths of its own being.

In the absence of external light, Jai's mind became the weaver of a grand tapestry, where stars fused and merged, giving birth to new constellations that had never before graced the night sky.

With each breath, the spectacle evolved, taking on ethereal hues and captivating Jai's senses. It was a testament to the incredible power of the mind to create illusions, to transcend the boundaries of what was known and venture into the realm of the extraordinary.

Within the depths of the cave, Jai marveled at this magical display, fully immersed in the dance of light and shadow, where reality and illusion entwined and blurred. The visionary spectacle served as a potent reminder of the profound influence of perception, where the mind could shape and mold the world, revealing hidden truths and leading one to question the very nature of existence.

PART TWO –
CHAPTER FOUR
Whispers in the Void

In the depths of the cave's embrace, Jai found themselves in a realm suspended between the waking world and the realm of dreams. The darkness enveloped them, a veil that blurred the boundaries of reality and imagination. As Jai sat in this enigmatic void, their mind ignited with a cascade of visions, like fragments of a dream woven into the fabric of their consciousness.

The visions unfolded before Jai's eyes, shifting and transforming, revealing scenes both familiar and fantastical. Faces and places, memories and fantasies merged into a kaleidoscope of fleeting images. It was as if their mind, liberated from the constraints of the physical realm, sought to explore the vast landscapes of the subconscious.

Time seemed to lose its hold as Jai traversed this realm, where the lines between past, present, and future dissolved into a harmonious tapestry. The whispers of forgotten stories resonated in the depths of their being, echoing through the cavernous expanse of the mind. In this state, Jai found themselves questioning the very nature of reality, for the visions were as vivid and tangible as any waking experience.

Amidst the swirling collage of memories, visions, faces, and places, one particular scene stood out from the tapestry of Jai's mind. It was a vivid recollection of a moment shared with the kind and gentle seaweed alchemist, Anaya, whom they had encountered in the search for their stollen belongings. The memory flooded Jai's senses, and a strange sensation washed over them, tinged with unease and familiarity.

In that recollection, Jai could hear Anaya's soothing voice recounting the enchanting tale of Daya, the clownfish. The story had resonated deeply within Jai, inspiring them to embrace a path of empathy and kindness. But now, as the memory played out before their mind's eye, an unsettling realization started to take hold.

Though Jai remembered meeting Anaya for the first time during their encounter, the sensation of familiarity tugged at their consciousness. It was as if Jai had known Anaya for far longer, as if their connection extended beyond the boundaries of that single encounter. The memory stirred a sense of closeness, as if Anaya held a significant place in Jai's life, more than just a chance encounter with a wise soul.

This realization puzzled Jai, and a myriad of questions swirled in their mind. How could this be? Had Jai and Anaya met before in some other realm or dimension? Or was this simply a trick of the mind, an illusion created by the enigmatic nature of the cave and the dreamscape it unveiled?

As Jai's mind continued to weave through the intricacies of their memories, another scene emerged with remarkable clarity—the encounter with the blacksmith, Kavi. The memory unfolded like a carefully scripted play, each detail etched into Jai's consciousness. But this time, a sense of familiarity enveloped Jai, casting a shadow of uncertainty over their understanding of reality.

The memory stirred a deep resonance within Jai's being, as if they had known Kavi far longer than the duration of their meeting on the day

Jai searched for their lost belongings. The connection felt profound, hinting at a bond that extended beyond the realm of chance encounters.

As the memory played out in Jai's mind, questions once again arose, echoing the perplexity of their earlier encounter with Anaya. How could it be that Jai felt such a deep sense of familiarity with Kavi, as if their destinies had been entwined long before their paths crossed? Was it possible that they had indeed met in some other realm or dimension, or was this another illusion woven by the enigmatic cave and its mystical powers?

Caught in the vortex of shifting memories, Jai's mind now wandered to the moment when they had traded the intricately carved butter tray to the humble baker. In the recollection, the tale unfolded just as it had been recounted—Jai's skillful craftsmanship, the exchange for a simple loaf of bread, and the baker's proclamation of the existence of the Moksha Vriksha. But amidst the memory, a nagging doubt began to seep into Jai's thoughts.

As Jai pondered the details of the butter tray, a flicker of uncertainty danced on the edges of their consciousness. It was a feeling that something was amiss, as if the threads of their own narrative were unraveling. The memory of carving the tray bore intricate patterns of lotus blooms and the sacred words "Moksha Vriksha". Yet, Jai couldn't recall the physical act of carving the tray itself. It was as if the artistic creation had slipped through their fingers, leaving only the lingering impression of the words they had chiseled into the wood.

A wave of confusion washed over Jai, amplifying the disquiet that had taken hold. Whispers, faint yet distinct, echoed through the depths of the cave, reverberating with an otherworldly presence. "Who are you?" the voice whispered, its ethereal timbre shrouded in mystery and intrigue. Jai's own voice seemed to mingle with the whispers, as if their very identity was being called into question.

The enigma deepened, and Jai's quest for self-discovery took on new layers of complexity. The illusions masking their true nature and purpose began to unravel, revealing glimpses of a greater truth that lay dormant within the recesses of their being. Who was Jai, truly, in the vast expanse of existence? And how had their journey become entangled in a web of illusions, blurring the boundaries between reality and imagination?

Jai's heart pounded in their chest, fear coursing through their veins like an electric current. The dissonance between their recollections and the reality they had known shattered their sense of stability. The haunting whispers persisted, merging with Jai's own voice, amplifying their anxiety and confusion.

Driven by a primal instinct to escape the enigmatic labyrinth of the cave, Jai's feet propelled them forward, their mind clouded with desperation. They sprinted through the seemingly endless passages, the darkness and uncertainty blurring their surroundings. But in their frenzied state, Jai failed to see the looming wall before them.

With a jarring impact, Jai collided with the unyielding stone barrier, their body crumpling in pain and disorientation. The collision knocked them into the ground, the world fading into a void of unconsciousness.

PART TWO – CHAPTER FIVE

Return to Mohendrapur

Jai's consciousness slowly resurfaced, a dull ache pulsating through their head. Their eyelids fluttered open, revealing the dimly lit cave still shrouded in mystery. As they struggled to sit up, a surge of disorientation washed over them, the remnants of their collision with the unforgiving wall. Gritting their teeth against the pain, Jai collected their waning strength and pushed themselves upright.

Leaning against the cave wall for support, Jai took a deep breath, filling their lungs with the cool, musty air. The familiar scents of damp earth enveloped them, reminding them of the path they had embarked upon. But now, a newfound determination burned within Jai, fueling their resolve to confront the enigmas that awaited them beyond the cave's embrace.

With a steady gait, Jai made their way back through the winding passages, their fingertips lightly grazing the rough stone walls as a guide. The darkness that once seemed intimidating now held a tinge of familiarity, as if the cave itself whispered its secrets to Jai, urging them forward.

Finally, Jai emerged from the cavern's mouth, blinking against the sudden onslaught of sunlight. The world outside greeted them with open arms, the sights and sounds of nature enveloping their senses. Taking a moment to reorient themselves, Jai set their gaze upon the distant horizon, where the city of Mohendrapur lay.

The journey back to the city was a trek filled with contemplation and introspection. Each step carried Jai closer to the place they once called home, a place they had left behind in search of something elusive—a journey that had led them to the depths of their own psyche. The memories of their encounters within the well and the cave intertwined with questions that demanded answers.

As the city's grand archway came into view, Jai's pace quickened with a mix of anticipation and apprehension. Mohendrapur, with its bustling streets and vibrant markets, held the key to unlocking the mysteries that had haunted Jai's mind. It was time to confront the illusions, face the truths that lay hidden beneath layers of denial and misconception.

As Jai ventured through the city's familiar alleys, a tumult of emotions engulfed them. The bustling streets, which once held comforting memories, now felt foreign and distant. Each passerby's gaze lingered on Jai, their eyes seemingly veiled with unspoken stories and quiet struggles. Yet, instead of being held back by the weight of those stares, Jai pressed forward, their heart pulsing with a clear and resolute purpose, as if propelled by an unseen force.

Jai's footsteps echoed with determination. The city's pulse intertwined with their own, creating a symphony of sound and motion. The energy of the streets coursed through their veins, propelling them forward with unwavering resolve.

Jai arrived at the blacksmith's shop, the clanging of metal filling the air. The sight of Kavi, adorned with soot-stained hands and a warm smile, brought a flicker of familiarity to Jai's eyes. Their gaze scanned the surroundings, taking in the sights and sounds that had once offered comfort and solace.

With a nod of acknowledgement, Kavi met Jai's gaze, unaware of the storm brewing within Jai's mind. The juxtaposition of the familiar scene and Jai's inner turmoil intensified the weight of their questions. It was in this moment that the conflicting emotions threatened to overflow, straining the fragile balance between Jai's perception of reality and the truth waiting to be unveiled.

Jai's voice trembled as they spoke, their words laced with urgency, "Do I know you? Have we crossed paths before our meeting in this realm?"

Confusion furrowed Kavi's brow as he tried to comprehend the intensity in Jai's voice. With a soothing tone, Kavi sought to alleviate the restlessness consuming Jai's mind, extending a gentle offer of a drink. "Have a drink, sit down, and tell me what's going on, Jai."

The tension in Jai's body heightened, their thoughts swirling in a whirlwind of uncertainty. In a moment of frustration, Jai lashed out, knocking the glass from Kavi's hand, the liquid shattering on the floor. The intensity of the scene grew, with shards of glass and emotions scattered across the room.

Jai stormed out of the blacksmith's shop, their heart pounding, their mind filled with a jumble of fragmented memories and unanswered questions. Anger and confusion consumed them as they paced through the streets, seeking solace in the chaos that surrounded them.

Driven by a restless determination, Jai's footsteps led them to the harbor, where the seaweed alchemist, Anaya, was known to reside. The salty scent of the ocean filled their nostrils as they approached her humble abode.

As Jai stepped into the threshold of Anaya's dwelling, their eyes met with a mixture of confusion and excitement. Anaya, embodied wisdom, and tranquility. Jai's heart fluttered with anticipation, hoping that within her presence, the pieces of their fragmented memories would align, and clarity would emerge.

Jai approached Anaya, their voice trembling with a mix of confusion and hope. "Anaya, I... I feel like I know you. But it's different this time. It's as if our connection runs deeper than I initially thought. Can you help me understand?"

Anaya's eyes held a knowing glimmer as she gently grasped Jai's hands. "What's wrong, my dear? Is it Kavi again?"

Jai's breath caught in their throat, surprise and bewilderment etching across their face. "You know Kavi. How do you know Kavi?"

Anaya looked at Jai with concern, her voice filled with genuine worry. "What do you mean? Kavi is our brother. We have known him our whole lives. Why does this disturb you so?"

Jai's mind raced, trying to reconcile the jigsaw pieces of their memories. "Kavi, the blacksmith?"

Anaya's eyes widened in alarm. "You're scaring me. What's going on? Why are you asking these questions?"

Jai's voice trembled as they struggled to make sense of the revelation. "He's... he's our brother?"

Anaya's expression softened, her voice filled with concern. "Yes, Kavi is our brother. What's happening? Did something occur between you two? Are you in trouble?"

A wave of emotions crashed over Jai as the truth unfolded before them. The realization that their forgotten memories were intricately tied to their sibling relationship left them stunned and disoriented. Questions swirled in their mind, and the depth of their journey became even more profound.

As Jai's mind grappled with the revelation of their forgotten memories and the newfound knowledge of their sibling connection, an overwhelming surge of emotions propelled them out of Anaya's dwelling. Jai's footsteps pounded against the city's streets as they sprinted with a sense of urgency, desperate to find solace in the place they had once called their temporary home.

Through the city's alleys and familiar corners, Jai's heart raced in sync with their racing thoughts. The scene where their belongings were stolen flashed in their mind, a painful reminder of the vulnerability and loss they had experienced. Ignoring the lingering traces of that past, Jai's gaze fixated on the distant river, a source of both solace and danger.

With each stride, Jai's determination grew stronger, fueled by a newfound purpose to rescue Mata from the perilous grasp of the river's currents. As they neared the water's edge, the sight of Mata struggling for survival sent a surge of adrenaline through Jai's veins. Without hesitation, Jai leaped into the icy embrace of the river, the chilling water enveloping their body.

But as Jai plunged into the depths, the realm of dreams once again took hold, as if the river had become a gateway between the two worlds. The sensation of water faded, replaced by the coolness of the cave floor beneath Jai's body. A jolt of awakening surged through their consciousness, and they found themselves back in the familiar embrace of the enigmatic cave.

Confusion washed over Jai as they blinked away the remnants of the dreamlike river rescue. They were back where it had all begun—the cave that held the whispers of forgotten stories, the cosmic dance of stars, and the mirage of memories. It was within this mystical space that the threads of their journey intertwined, leading them closer to the truths that lay buried within.

PART TWO -
CHAPTER SIX
Threads of Perception

As Jai's eyelids fluttered open, the dimly lit cave greeted them with its whispers. The weight of the revelations from the dream still clung to their consciousness, like an intricate web of fragmented memories. The realization that Kavi and Anaya were their siblings echoed through Jai's mind, shattering illusions they had constructed. With each passing moment, the fragments of their once-believed reality fell away, revealing a stark truth they were unprepared to face.

Pushing themselves up from the cold cave floor, Jai steadied their trembling legs and took a deep breath. The cave walls, once a comforting sanctuary, now seemed like a cage of illusions, imprisoning them in a false narrative. The time for truth had come, and Jai knew they had to seek guidance outside the confines of this enigmatic place.

Leaving the cave behind, Jai emerged into the daylight, squinting against the sudden brightness. The world outside awaited them, a blank canvas upon which their true story would be painted. With each step, determination grew in Jai's heart, fueled by a burning desire to unravel the mysteries that had shaped their existence.

Guided by an inner compass, Jai set out on the journey to find the hermit, whose wisdom and knowledge could serve as a beacon in the darkness. The path ahead was unknown, strewn with doubts and uncertainties, but Jai refused to falter. They would confront their past, confront their own illusions, and find a way to embrace the truth that lay hidden beneath the layers of deceit.

Through dense forests and winding trails, Jai's footsteps echoed the resolute rhythm of their quest. As the sun cast its glow upon the world, Jai's determination grew stronger, illuminating the path ahead. Hours turned into days, and still, Jai pressed on, their mind consumed by thoughts of who they truly were and how their life had diverged from reality.

Jai stood before the hermit's dwelling, their heart pounding in their chest. They raised their fist, prepared to knock on the door and seek solace in the hermit's wisdom. However, before Jai could make contact with the weathered wood, the door swung open as if anticipating their arrival.

Startled, Jai's hand froze in mid-air, and their eyes widened with surprise. The hermit stood in the doorway, their serene gaze meeting Jai's with an uncanny knowing. It was as if the hermit had sensed Jai's presence even before they had approached.

With a gentle smile, the hermit stepped out, the folds of their tattered robe swaying in the breeze. "What troubles your spirit, my child?" they asked, their voice carrying the weight of compassion and ancient wisdom.

Jai's voice quivered, a mixture of vulnerability and determination. "I seek the truth, wise one. The truth of who I am and how my life has become a tapestry of illusions."

The hermit's eyes softened, their gaze filled with compassion. They placed a hand on Jai's shoulder, offering reassurance. "Fear not, my child, for the path to truth can be both daunting and liberating. Let us embark on a walk through the forest, where nature's serenity can help calm your restless spirit."

Jai nodded, gratitude welling up within them for the hermit's understanding. As they ventured into the lush greenery, a sense of tranquility enveloped Jai's being. The hermit's presence acted as an anchor, grounding them amidst the swirling uncertainties.

With each step, the forest whispered its secrets to Jai, as if sharing ancient wisdom long forgotten. The dappled sunlight filtered through the canopy, casting dancing shadows on the forest floor. Jai's senses heightened, attuned to the subtle sounds of rustling leaves and the sweet fragrance of wildflowers.

As they walked, the hermit encouraged Jai to immerse themselves in the present moment, to let go of the weight of past illusions and embrace the possibilities of the unknown. They pointed out the intricate patterns carved by time on the gnarled tree trunks, reminding Jai of the resilience that comes from weathering life's storms.

In the distance, a magnificent sight caught their attention. A cascading waterfall, framed by lush foliage, glistened under the gentle sunlight. Its roaring sound filled the air, creating a symphony of nature's power.

Jai's heart skipped a beat, drawn to the majestic beauty before them. Eagerly, they quickened their pace, the anticipation growing with each step. The rhythmic sound of rushing water grew louder, pulling them closer to the enchanting spectacle.

As Jai approached, the waterfall seemed to shimmer and waver, as if teasing them from afar. With every stride, the grandeur of the waterfall receded, dissolving into thin air until it vanished entirely. Jai's eyes widened with surprise and confusion. "Where did it go?" Jai asked, bewildered.

The hermit, who had caught up to Jai, stood beside them, a serene smile gracing their face. They pointed to the interplay of sunlight filtering through the dense canopy, casting intricate patterns on the cliff face where the waterfall had once appeared.

"Behold, Jai," the hermit said, their voice filled with gentle wisdom. "The sun's rays, filtered through the forest's embrace, create a captivating optical illusion. The light dances upon the cliff, conjuring the image of a waterfall where there is none."

Jai's astonishment turned into fascination as they observed the phenomenon. The shifting patterns of light and shadow painted a vivid mirage, deceiving their eyes and awakening their understanding of the illusions that nature can weave.

"The world around us is full of wonders, Jai," the hermit continued. "Sometimes, what we perceive is not always what truly exists. These illusions serve as a reminder to look beyond the surface, to question and seek a deeper understanding."

As Jai and the hermit ventured deeper into the forest, their steps guided by curiosity and reflection, they stumbled upon a patch of soft earth adorned with delicate footprints. The imprints, captured their attention, compelling them to pause and contemplate their meaning.

Jai's eyes widened in recognition, a spark of realization igniting within their being. "Hermit, look," Jai exclaimed, pointing at the distinct footprints etched in the ground. "These footprints must be ours. I can discern the familiar shape of my shoes and the pattern of your sandals."

The hermit, deeply attuned to the interconnectedness of all things, nodded in agreement, his eyes reflecting the wisdom of ages. "Indeed, Jai," he responded with a serene smile. "These footprints bear the freshness of recent passage. The softness of the soil and the delicate traces of rain reveal their presence in the present moment, untouched by the eroding hands of time."

Intrigued by the profound implications, Jai couldn't help but inquire further, their voice resonating with curiosity. "What, then, is the lesson hidden within these fleeting imprints?" they asked, their eagerness palpable.

The hermit paused, allowing the significance of their surroundings to sink in, before offering his profound insight. "Just as the mirage deceives our eyes, these footprints serve as a profound reminder of the transient nature of all phenomena," he replied, his words carrying a weight of truth. "Life unfurls as an intricate dance, where what once appeared solid and certain can dissolve in the blink of an eye."

Captivated by the wisdom flowing from the hermit's words, Jai's gaze shifted upwards to the canopy above. Sunbeams pierced through the dense foliage, casting a mesmerizing spectacle of dancing light and shadows upon the forest floor. The interplay of brightness and darkness created an enchanting mosaic, constantly shifting and evolving.

The hermit, attuned to the ephemeral nature of existence, followed Jai's gaze and smiled knowingly. "Behold the dance of sunbeams," he whispered, his voice carrying a sense of reverence. "In this ever-changing play of light and shadow, we witness the profound truth of reality's transience."

"What appears solid and immutable is but a dance of light and darkness," Jai murmured, their voice tinged with awe. "It is a reflection of the illusory nature of our material existence. We are woven into this intricate tapestry of impermanence."

The hermit nodded, acknowledging Jai's newfound understanding. "Indeed, my dear Jai," he replied, his voice filled with warmth. "The dance of sunbeams reminds us that what we perceive as solid and unchanging is, in reality, a ceaseless flow of energy and form. The material world, like these transient patterns of light, is but a fleeting expression of a deeper reality."

Jai's eyes were drawn to a lush bush adorned with vibrant leaves. Amidst the foliage, they spotted a chameleon, its body perfectly synchronized with the surrounding hues. It was as if the creature possessed the innate ability to merge with its environment, becoming one with the tapestry of colors.

The hermit gently directed Jai's attention to the chameleon, a knowing smile gracing his face. "Observe, dear Jai," he whispered, his voice carrying the weight of ancient wisdom. "The chameleon's remarkable camouflage serves as a metaphor for the grand illusion that veils our perception."

Jai's gaze remained fixed on the mesmerizing sight before them. The chameleon effortlessly shifted its colors, adapting to the ever-changing backdrop. It was a living testament to the deceptive nature of appearances and the malleability of forms.

"The chameleon teaches us that what we perceive is not always what truly exists," the hermit continued, his voice tinged with a gentle reverence. "Just as this creature seamlessly blends with its surroundings, our perception of reality is shaped by our ever-changing perspectives and the illusions woven by our senses."

As Jai and the hermit continued their sojourn through the forest, their footsteps led them to a wondrous sight—a delicate butterfly in the midst of its metamorphic journey. They watched in awe as the creature gracefully emerged from its chrysalis, its once-bound form now unfurling into vibrant wings.

The hermit's eyes sparkled with profound insight, sensing the significance of this transformative moment. "Behold, dear Jai," he whispered, his voice filled with reverence. "The butterfly's metamorphosis serves as a poignant reminder of the illusory nature of identity and the perpetual dance of change that permeates all of existence."

Jai's gaze remained fixed on the butterfly, their heart swelling with wonder. They witnessed the creature's graceful transition from one form to another, shedding the confines of its former self to embrace newfound beauty and freedom. It was a testament to the inherent impermanence of life and the endless possibilities for growth and renewal.

"The butterfly's journey mirrors our own path," the hermit explained, his voice carrying the weight of ancient wisdom. "Just as this ethereal creature discards its old identity, we too have the capacity to transform, to evolve beyond the limitations of our past selves."

Jai's mind danced with newfound understanding. They realized that their previous attachments to a fixed sense of identity were merely illusions, veils that obscured the boundless potential within. Like the butterfly, they too were capable of embracing the ever-changing nature of existence, releasing the constraints of what they once thought defined them.

"The butterfly teaches us that change is not to be feared but embraced," the hermit whispered. "It reveals the beauty that lies in letting go, in surrendering to the currents of transformation that flow through our lives."

PART TWO –
CHAPTER SEVEN
Veils of Denial

As Jai and the hermit ventured through the dense forest, their footsteps hushed by the carpet of fallen leaves, they stumbled upon a serene and tranquil lake nestled amidst the towering trees. The air carried a sense of stillness, and the water's surface reflected the peaceful surroundings, creating a mirror-like expanse that beckoned them closer.

Intrigued by the enigmatic allure of the lake, Jai's curiosity grew with every step. Their heart fluttered with anticipation as they approached the water's edge, expecting to witness a clear reflection of their being. But to their surprise, the image that greeted them was anything but true.

Jai's reflection appeared distorted and fragmented, as if the very essence of their existence had been scattered and rearranged. The waters seemed to play tricks on their perception, dancing with the boundaries of reality.

Puzzled and yearning for understanding, Jai turned to the hermit, their eyes searching for answers in the depths of the hermit's gaze. The hermit, with eyes that held a hint of sorrow, spoke in a voice that resonated with wisdom and compassion.

"This lake, dear Jai, holds a profound metaphor for the illusions we weave through the veil of denial," the hermit said, their words carrying the weight of introspection. "It reflects not only what we see but also what we choose to acknowledge or ignore."

Jai's brows furrowed, their mind a whirlwind of thoughts and questions. They listened intently as the hermit continued, their voice gentle yet tinged with a bittersweet truth.

"Denial, like the distortion of your reflection, is a shield we construct to protect ourselves from the harsh glare of painful truths," the hermit explained. "It creates a realm of illusions, where reality becomes blurred and fragments of our existence are rearranged to fit a narrative of comfort."

With newfound awareness guiding their every step, Jai and the hermit continued their journey through the forest. The dappled sunlight filtered through the canopy, casting enchanting patterns of light and shadow upon the forest floor. It was as if the dance of illumination beckoned them further, inviting them to embrace the truths that lay hidden within the depths of the woods.

As they ventured deeper into the forest, their path led them to an unexpected encounter. Through the foliage, Jai caught a glimpse of two familiar figures—boys they had encountered before, the very ones who had taken Jai's possessions. In that moment, their hearts swelled with a mixture of curiosity, compassion, and a desire for reconciliation.

Drawing closer, Jai discovered the boys, accompanied by their father, trying to make art amidst the serene ambience of nature. The struggle was evident in their furrowed brows and frustrated expressions. It was a poignant reminder of their own journey and the obstacles they had overcome to pursue their artistic path.

The hermit, sensing the opportunity for growth and healing, whispered to Jai, suggesting that they offer the boys some guidance and support. Jai understood the significance of this moment, a chance to extend a hand of forgiveness, empathy, and mentorship.

Approaching the boys with a calm and supportive presence, Jai shared their artistic insights and techniques, hoping to inspire and guide them through their creative process. But to Jai's surprise, their attempts to offer assistance fell short.

As Jai struggled to make art and offer any meaningful suggestions to the boys, frustration and confusion mounted within them. The weight of their inability to create weighed heavily on their spirit, and they turned to the hermit, seeking solace and understanding.

Jai poured out their frustrations, their voice tinged with a mix of despair and confusion. "Why can't I make art? What is wrong with me?" Jai pleaded, their eyes searching the hermit's for answers.

The hermit, ever wise and perceptive, studied Jai intently, their gaze filled with compassion. "Dear Jai," the hermit began gently, "sometimes, the truth we seek lies not in the realm of what we can do, but in accepting what we cannot."

Confusion etched deeper into Jai's furrowed brow as they tried to comprehend the hermit's words. The hermit continued, their voice steady and patient, "It is possible, dear one, that your struggle to create art stems from the fact that you are not an artisan yourself." The words hung in the air, heavy with revelation.

Jai's breath caught in their throat as fragments of memories, buried deep within their consciousness, began to resurface. The hermit's words began to unlock a truth Jai had long denied—the art that they had pursued was not their own, but a tribute to a loved one lost.

A flood of emotions overwhelmed Jai—a mix of grief, loss, and the weight of denial that they had carried for so long. It became clear that the stolen items the boys possessed were not just random creations, but remnants of Jai's significant other, Mata, the true artisan and poet whose talent had breathed life into those pieces.

In the agonizing wake of losing their beloved, Jai began weaving a protective tapestry of minor deceptions—small, seemingly harmless lies that provided fleeting moments of comfort. But as time progressed and their mental well-being deteriorated, these fibs intertwined, growing denser and more elaborate, until they formed a suffocating web of falsehoods. Without even fully realizing, Jai had submerged themselves into this illusory realm, mistakenly adopting the identity of an artist. In this crafted mirage, they found solace, sheltering their wounded heart by presenting Mata's masterpieces as their own creations.

Tears welled up in Jai's eyes as the realization washed over them. The hermit, ever gentle, reached out a comforting hand, offering solace in the face of this painful truth. "Dear Jai, it takes great strength to confront our fears and face the truth that lies beneath. This revelation is an opportunity for healing and growth."

Before Jai could respond, a sudden tense stillness descended upon the clearing. The father, having observed the exchange between Jai and the hermit, and sensing the raw emotions pouring forth from Jai, took swift action. His protective instincts flared, seeing in Jai not the traveling artist he once believed, but a broken individual who was grappling with the depth of their own delusion.

Without a word, he motioned for the boys to gather their things, his eyes never leaving Jai's. His gaze held a mixture of pity, caution, and fear.

110

His actions were clear — Jai was no longer someone he wanted his children to associate with.

With a heavy heart, Jai watched as the boys' father instinctively grabbed their hands and led them away, deeper into the forest. A mixture of confusion and concern clouded Jai's thoughts, and they turned to the hermit, seeking answers amidst the emotional storm.

"What's happening?" Jai's voice quivered, their eyes following the father and boys as they disappeared among the trees. "Why does he steer them away from me?" Jai's heart ached, knowing that their own pain had inadvertently caused discomfort and misunderstanding.

Jai's emotions spiraled out of control, engulfed in a maelstrom of confusion and despair. The weight of their revelations bore heavily upon them, causing an overwhelming surge of panic. Doubt gnawed at the edges of their mind, whispering that perhaps they had descended into madness.

Sensing Jai's distress, the hermit extended a gentle hand, attempting to calm their racing thoughts. "Breathe, Jai," the hermit urged softly. "Remember the waterfall, the mirage that vanished as we drew closer. The truth can be elusive, but it is not a fabrication of your mind. Embrace the uncertainty and trust in your journey."

But Jai's anguish fueled their frantic actions. Ignoring the hermit's plea, they sprinted towards the boys and their father, driven by an overwhelming need to connect, to reclaim the stolen fragments of their existence. Jai sprinted through the forest, and in their haste, failed to notice the towering tree standing defiantly in their path.

With a resounding thud, Jai collided with the unyielding trunk. Pain radiated through their body, and darkness consumed their sight as they tumbled into the depths of unconsciousness.

As Jai opened their eyes, they found themselves in the depths of the cave. The darkness surrounded them, a cloak of uncertainty that whispered of hidden truths.

The air hung heavy with a stillness, and a sense of mystery permeated the cavernous space. Jai's gaze wandered, searching for any hint of light, any glimmer of guidance that could lead them out of the enigmatic depths.

In the distance, a faint glow teased the edges of their vision, whispering promises of illumination and escape. Cautiously hopeful, Jai rose to their feet, their movements tentative in the pitch-black void. With each step, the cave walls seemed to murmur secrets and echoes of forgotten tales, leaving Jai to question the very nature of their reality.

The path ahead was shrouded in uncertainty, yet an unyielding determination compelled Jai to press onward. Their outstretched hands grazed the rough contours of the cave, seeking reassurance and stability in the touch of stone.

The glimmer of light grew brighter, casting shadows that danced upon the cave walls. In that fragile illumination, Jai glimpsed faint traces of ancient markings and hidden wisdom, evoking a sense of reverence for the enigma of existence and a connection to those who walked here before them.

With each step closer to the source of light, the glow intensified, illuminating Jai's path and dispelling the remnants of darkness. The cave's mouth opened wide, revealing a breathtaking sight—a world adorned in the splendor of a new day.

As Jai stepped into the embrace of sunlight, a gentle breeze brushed against their skin, carrying the invigorating scent of blooming flowers.

The vibrant hues of nature painted a tapestry of life, filling their senses with a renewed vitality.

In that moment, as if in perfect harmony with the universe, a delicate butterfly alighted upon Jai's outstretched hand. Its wings, adorned with intricate patterns of iridescent colors, seemed to carry a message from the natural world—a message of transformation, resilience, and the interconnectedness of all living beings.

Jai marveled at the butterfly's grace, its presence a symbol of the profound cycles of life and the enduring spirit of metamorphosis. In that fleeting encounter, Jai felt a sense of oneness with the world, as if they too had emerged from the depths of their own personal cocoon, ready to embrace the possibilities that lay ahead.

PART TWO -
EPILOGUE
Silent Awakening

"In the hush of silence, peace is sown,
A sanctuary for the soul to own.
Amid life's chaos, a tranquil balm,
In quietude, we find our calm."

        -Mata

Jai returned to the Refuge of Inner Stillness, their footsteps echoing softly in the hallowed space. Within the sanctity of Mauna, the vow of silence enveloped them, withholding the revelation of their transformative journey in the cave.

In this realm of stillness, Jai embraced the rhythm of daily chores and situations that unfolded around them, each carrying profound echoes of the lessons they encountered.

The practice of asana had become an anchor for Jai, an intimate dance of breath and movement. From the initial stages of physical recovery to the blossoming of strength and flexibility, Jai had discovered deeper truths of this ancient discipline. The sages had imparted wisdom, revealing that the ultimate goal of asana was to prepare the mind and body for the realms of meditation.

In the depths of the Refuge, where silence reigned supreme, Jai ventured into the realm of breathwork. With the guidance of the sages, Jai embarked on a profound exploration of pranayama. Each inhalation and exhalation carried them deeper within, dissolving tensions and shedding layers of conditioning. In this inner sanctuary, Jai's awareness of the intimate connection between breath and subtle energies expanded.

Days turned into weeks, and weeks into months as Jai continued their silent existence within the Refuge. Amidst the tapestry of communal living, they witnessed the complexities of human interactions, the joys, and challenges of shared silence. Through these observations, Jai gleaned profound insights into the nature of relationships, compassion, and the importance of mindful communication.

Time flowed like a silent river, nurturing Jai's mental and emotional well-being, and instilling a deep sense of calm that radiated from within. As the seasons passed, Jai's transformation unfolded, and the veil of delusion that had shrouded their perception began to lift.

In the dim recesses of the cave, where darkness cloaked the senses, Jai journeyed into the depths of their own mind. Without external distractions, they confronted the il lusions that had ensnared them. Within the void of sensory deprivation, Jai's projections and delusions were stripped bare, leaving only the raw truth waiting to be acknowledged.

116

The time came when Jai and the sages embarked on their sacred pilgrimage to the Sanctuary of Whispers—a haven nestled beneath the grand canopy of the bayan tree. Within its sheltering embrace, the veil of silence was lifted, and Jai found their voice once more.

With calm serenity, Jai shared the profound awakening that had unfolded within the cave. They spoke of the loss that had led them astray, the passing of their beloved Mata, and the subsequent spiral into delusion and denial. They spoke of the illusions that had driven their desperate search for the Moksha Vriksha tree.

As their words filled the air, Jai's voice resonated with newfound clarity. "I can see now," they declared. "I am no longer imprisoned by my own delusion."

It was within this revelation that Jai dared to question the existence of the Moksha Vriksha itself. They expressed their newfound understanding that the search for this tree was but another facet of their own illusion—a false truth that had perpetuated their cycle of denial.

However, before their words could fully settle, a sage interjected with gentle authority. Their voice carried wisdom. They explained that the Moksha Vriksha was indeed real—a sacred tree holding the key to healing, self-discovery, and ultimate liberation. The sage recounted their own transformative encounter with the tree, emphasizing its profound impact on their journey.

Jai prepared to depart from the sages, their heart weighed heavy with a mixture of gratitude and anticipation. The sages had entrusted them with sacred instructions that would serve as their guide on the path to the Moksha Vriksha.

Jai paused their departure as a spirited exchange unfolded among the sages, revealing the extraordinary nature of the hermit who had left an indelible mark on Jai's journey.

"He's no ordinary hermit," remarked one sage with a mischievous twinkle in their eye.

Jai's curiosity piqued, and they eagerly asked, "Who is he, then?"

"He's a sage," another sage proclaimed, their voice tinged with awe.

A grin spread across the face of the third sage as they replied, "Oh, and he's no ordinary sage!"

Intrigued, Jai leaned in closer, anticipating the revelations to come. "What sets him apart?"

"He's a scribe," the fourth sage announced with a playful wink.

The sages exchanged knowing glances.

"Yes, and he's no ordinary scribe," the first sage declared, their voice brimming with excitement.

A mischievous smile danced upon the lips of the second sage. "His writings will change the world."

The third sage nodded; their eyes gleaming with reverence. "And his work will be spoken of for thousands of years to come."

The first sage gently interjected, a twinkle in their eye. "Ah, and it is not only his work that will echo through time. It is the work we're doing together."

Jai's breath caught in their throat, their gaze shifting from one sage to another. The realization washed over them like a gentle wave, connecting them to a shared purpose that transcended individual journeys. A profound sense of belonging and unity settled within Jai's being. They were part of something greater—a collective tapestry of wisdom and transformation that would ripple through generations.

With this newfound understanding, Jai bid farewell to the sages, carrying the weight of their collective mission in their heart. As they embarked on their solitary journey, guided by the sacred instructions and inspired by the extraordinary nature of the hermit and the sages, Jai felt a renewed sense of purpose.

The path ahead shimmered with possibility and the promise of profound discovery. The search for the Moksha Vriksha—a tree that held the key to healing, self-discovery, and ultimate liberation—became not just a personal quest but a testament to the interconnectedness of all beings and the timeless nature of wisdom.

Part 3

Traversing the Winding Path

PART THREE - PROLOGUE
The Escape of Kiran

In a time of wealth and privilege, there lived a dog named Kiran. Adorned in a coat of ebony and gold, they were the cherished pet of a wealthy family. But within the walls of their opulent abode, Kiran yearned for a taste of freedom beyond the confinements of their privileged existence.

One fateful day, as the sun cast its golden rays upon the palace grounds, Kiran's restless spirit could no longer be contained. With a determined heart and a burning desire for liberation, they made a daring decision—to escape the gilded cage that had become their home.

Under the cloak of night, when the moon shone brightly in the sky, Kiran seized the opportunity to slip away unnoticed. They darted through the palace corridors, their paws silent against the marble floors.

With each step, the weight of captivity grew lighter, and the allure of the outside world beckoned. As they emerged into the open air, the city's vibrant energy enveloped Kiran. The scent of adventure wafted through the streets, mingling with the sounds of bustling markets and distant laughter. Kiran's heartbeat with excitement as they embarked on a journey into the unknown.

Through narrow alleyways and winding paths, Kiran traversed the cityscape, their senses heightened by the sights, sounds, and scents of a world previously unknown. They became a nomad, guided by an inner compass that led them toward the vast horizons beyond the palace walls.

Kiran ran through the city, their paws carried them further into the wilderness, leaving the familiar behind. The towering buildings and bustling streets gave way to a dense forest, where nature's symphony played in harmony.

In the heart of the forest, surrounded by towering trees and a canopy of leaves, Kiran found themselves alone, their breath visible in the cold air. Fear began to creep into their thoughts, mirroring the chill that gripped their body. But just as despair threatened to take hold, a hoot pierced the silence of the night.

Kiran's gaze shifted upward, meeting the penetrating eyes of the wise owl perched on a branch above. There was a profound connection in that moment, an unspoken understanding that transcended the boundaries of language. Through the language of the soul, the owl conveyed a message of guidance and reassurance.

With a gentle flapping of its wings, the owl took flight, gliding through the moonlit forest. Kiran, instinctively recognizing the owl's intent, followed with unwavering determination. The hoots echoed through the night, leading Kiran deeper into the wilderness.

The owl's calls guided Kiran with a rhythmic dance, beckoning them forward through the winding paths of the forest. With each hoot, a sense of trust and security grew within Kiran's heart. It was as if the owl's presence infused them with a renewed sense of purpose and a reminder that they were not alone on this journey.

The chase continued, the distance between Kiran and the owl gradually diminishing. The hoots grew louder, guiding Kiran to a hidden sanctuary—a cave nestled amidst the ancient rocks. As Kiran entered the sacred space, a sense of peace washed over them, and the fear that once gripped their heart began to melt away.

In the embrace of the cave, Kiran found solace and warmth. The darkness became a sanctuary, shielding them from the harshness of the external world. Here, in this tranquil refuge, they could find respite, regaining their strength and composure.

As the first rays of sunlight pierced through the cracks of the cave, Kiran stirred from their slumber, awakened by the gentle touch of dawn. The world outside beckoned once again, and Kiran knew it was time to continue their journey.

Leaving the sanctuary of the cave behind, Kiran ventured forth into the renewed day. The forest embraced them with open arms, its ancient trees whispering secrets of resilience and growth. They walked with purpose, guided by an invisible thread of destiny that had woven itself through their being.

Hours turned into moments as Kiran roamed through the wilderness, their senses attuned to the subtle nuances of nature. The symphony of chirping birds and rustling leaves echoed in their ears, a reminder of the interconnectedness of all living beings.

As twilight painted the sky in hues of orange and purple, Kiran found themselves in a clearing, a soft carpet of grass beneath their paws. It was there, in that serene space, that they encountered a tortoise, slowly ambling across the path.

Though Kiran initially passed by the tortoise, their journey through the forest took an unexpected turn as night descended upon them. The dog's paws hesitated, sensing the encroaching darkness and feeling a sense of vulnerability. They longed for companionship, a presence to ward off the shadows that danced around them.

As darkness enveloped the forest, Kiran's heart pounded with fear and uncertainty. With a yearning desire to dispel the loneliness, Kiran retraced their steps, returning to the very spot where they had first encountered the tortoise.

The tortoise, with its unhurried movements, offered a sense of solace, a comforting presence in the vastness of the forest. The tortoise, unperturbed by Kiran's distress, sat still without offering any solace. Frustration welled up within Kiran, desperate for some form of connection or guidance in this daunting situation.

In a state of heightened agitation, Kiran tried to communicate with the tortoise, their barks and whimpers echoing through the stillness of the night. But the tortoise remained unmoved, its ancient gaze fixed ahead, seemingly indifferent to Kiran's distress.

Frustration turned into weariness, and exhaustion washed over Kiran's trembling body. Seeking respite, Kiran instinctively settled down beside the tortoise, seeking solace in its grounded presence. The dog's breath gradually steadied, and as if mirroring the tortoise's serenity, Kiran slipped into an unintended state of calm.

The restless thoughts and fears that had plagued Kiran slowly dissolved, replaced by a tranquil stillness. In this unexpected moment of surrender, Kiran found temporary relief from their overwhelming emotions. In the embrace of sleep, the dog's body relaxed, and a sense of peace settled over them, even in the midst of the unknown.

The tortoise, steadfast and unresponsive, remained a silent witness to Kiran's journey from fear to momentary tranquility. Their encounter, although devoid of explicit communication, held a subtle resonance, teaching Kiran the power of finding stillness within oneself, even in the most chaotic of circumstances.

As the first light of dawn painted the sky in gentle hues, Kiran awoke from their slumber, feeling a lingering sense of calmness from their encounter with the tortoise. Renewed and determined, they resumed their journey through the dense forest, their senses attuned to every sound and scent.

Guided by an innate intuition, Kiran followed the subtle whispers of their instincts. Step by step, they ventured deeper into the heart of the forest, until they reached the edge of a precipice. There, poised on the brink of a magnificent waterfall, was a swan—a vision of elegance and grace.

The swan sat serenely on the calm waters above the cascading falls, its pure white feathers shimmering in the soft sunlight. Kiran stood mesmerized by the sight, a newfound stillness settling within their being. It was as if time stood still, and all that existed in that moment was the ethereal presence of the swan.

In the tranquil dance between water and air, Kiran felt an invisible thread connecting them to the swan—a profound sense of unity and harmony. The swan, unperturbed by Kiran's presence, radiated an aura of tranquility and grace, inviting Kiran to drink from the well of serenity it embodied.

With awe and reverence, Kiran gazed upon the swan, absorbing its presence like a sponge. The dog's own restlessness began to dissolve, replaced by a deep sense of peace. In the swan's reflection on the still waters, Kiran caught a glimpse of their own potential for inner peace.

As Kiran stood there, captivated by the swan's ethereal presence, a sense of serenity enveloped them. It was as if time stood still, and the world around them faded into the background. Lost in a trance-like state, Kiran took a step forward, unaware of the perilous edge that awaited them.

In a moment of both grace and folly, the dog, carried away by the sheer force of their newfound tranquility, gently and foolishly stepped off the cliff. Their descent through the air was both exhilarating and terrifying, a rush of wind against their fur as they plunged downward.

As Kiran plummeted through the air, the deafening roar of the waterfall echoed in their ears, drowning out all other sounds. The jagged rocks below loomed closer, a menacing threat that could shatter their existence in an instant.

PART THREE - CHAPTER ONE
Currents of Connection

Jai sought refuge within the shelter of a makeshift dwelling nestled deep in the heart of the forest. Their body, weary from the day's arduous journey, yearned for solace. The cool night air tenderly caressed their face, carrying with it a symphony of whispered melodies from the natural world. As Jai settled in, a gentle hoot pierced through the stillness, harmonizing with the rustling leaves and the distant calls of nocturnal creatures.

Settling into a state of deep relaxation, Jai embraced the present moment, allowing their breath to slow and their senses to attune to the gentle symphony of the forest. The hoot of the owl, a fleeting melody in the vast expanse of the night, carried with it a subtle reminder of the interconnectedness of all beings.

Wrapped in a cloak of stillness and gratitude, Jai's consciousness expanded, blending with the ancient wisdom of the forest. The owl's hoot, a distant echo in the tapestry of existence, faded into the background as Jai surrendered to the embrace of slumber.

Jai awoke with the first light of dawn, their body rejuvenated by a restful night's sleep. They emerged from their shelter, feeling a renewed sense of purpose coursing through their veins. The instructions of the sage echoed in their mind, guiding their every step towards the sacred Moksha Vriksha tree.

With unwavering determination, Jai embarked on the next leg of their journey, traversing the winding path that stretched before them. Step by step, they followed the sage's guidance, their senses attuned to the whispers of the forest.

After a considerable time, Jai's eyes fell upon a peculiar sight—a tortoise, nestled in the tranquility of meditation. The tortoise's stillness captivated Jai, an embodiment of profound contemplation amidst the ever-changing tapestry of life.

As instructed by the sage, Jai approached the meditating tortoise with reverence, their gaze meeting the steady presence of the creature. In that moment of silent connection, a silent exchange unfolded—an unspoken acknowledgment of the tortoise's innate wisdom.

With a heart filled with gratitude, Jai followed the sage's instruction to turn their gaze towards the nearest mountain peak. A sense of anticipation grew within them as they set their sights on the towering ridge, a testament to nature's grandeur.

The path leading to the mountain peak seemed treacherous, dotted with rocks and steep inclines. Yet, fueled by their unwavering determination and guided by the sage's wisdom, Jai pressed on. Each step brought them closer to the elusive Moksha Vriksha tree.

The ascent demanded focus and resilience. Jai's mind became attuned to the present moment, honing in on the rhythm of their footsteps, the beating of their heart, and the whispers of the wind. They felt a profound connection to the natural world, recognizing their place within the vast tapestry of existence.

Jai sat at the opening of the cave, the vibrant colors of the setting sun painting the sky in hues of orange and pink. The cool breeze brushed against their skin, carrying with it the gentle whispers of the wind. With crossed legs and closed eyes, they attempted to quiet their racing thoughts and delve into the depths of meditation.

As Jai focused on their breath, they couldn't help but feel a sense of frustration. Doubts crept into their mind, questioning whether they were truly meditating correctly. They had watched the sages meditate for countless hours, but wondered if their own experience resembled that of the sage's.

Unable to find immediate answers, Jai decided to release their concerns and seek solace in the comforting embrace of the cave. With a gentle sigh, they closed their eyes and allowed themselves to surrender to the serenity of the surroundings.

The cool, damp air of the cave enveloped Jai, cradling them in a sense of tranquility. Soft echoes of their breath reverberated against the cave walls, creating a soothing rhythm that lulled their weary mind and body.

As they settled into the cave's embrace, a profound stillness washed over Jai, soothing their restless thoughts. The worries and uncertainties that had troubled them moments before began to dissipate, replaced by a deep sense of peace and surrender.

Wrapped in the gentle darkness of the cave, Jai found comfort in the silence that surrounded them. The symphony of their breath and the steady beat of their heart became the only sounds in their awareness, merging with the subtle echoes of nature outside

As the night gradually gave way to the soft hues of dawn, a gentle ray of sunlight pierced through the mouth of the cave, casting a warm glow upon Jai's peaceful form. Sensing the arrival of a new day, Jai slowly awakened from their restful slumber.

Stretching their limbs and allowing the last remnants of sleep to fade away, Jai felt a renewed sense of energy coursing through their body. They sat up, their senses fully attuned to the tranquility that enveloped the cave.

With a calm and centered mind, Jai found a serene spot just outside the mouth of the cave. The natural beauty that surrounded them served as a backdrop, infusing their practice with a sense of harmony and connection.

In this tranquil setting, Jai grounded themselves on the earth, feeling the coolness of the ground beneath their feet. They closed their eyes, turning their attention inward and immersing themselves in the symphony of their breath.

Moving with grace and intention, Jai flowed from one yoga pose to another. Their body became a vessel of ancient wisdom, as if echoing the countless souls who had sought enlightenment in these very lands. The rustling leaves provided a natural soundtrack, harmonizing with the rhythm of their movements.

As the morning sunlight filtered through the trees, Jai basked in its gentle warmth, feeling its energy infuse their being as they moved through their yoga practice. They surrendered to the flow of their poses, guided by an innate knowing of their body.

The ancient trees stood as silent witnesses, emanating a sense of wisdom and resilience. Jai felt their presence, drawing inspiration from their unwavering strength and deep-rooted connection to the earth. With each breath, Jai cultivated a profound sense of unity with the natural world. The forest whispered secrets of interconnectedness, reminding them that they were but a small part of a vast and intricate tapestry of existence.

As they rounded a bend in the forest path, Jai's eyes widened in awe. Before them cascaded a majestic waterfall, its pristine waters gushing forth with unyielding power. The sight filled Jai's heart with a sense of reverence and wonder.

Drawn to the ethereal beauty of the falls, Jai found a place to sit at the bottom, where the water gently caressed their feet. The sound of rushing water mingled with the symphony of their breath, creating a harmonious melody that resonated within.

In this sacred space, Jai surrendered to the timeless rhythm of nature. The mist from the waterfall kissed their skin, invigorating their senses and immersing them in a tranquil state of being.

As Jai closed their eyes, the roar of the falls faded into the background, replaced by a deep stillness that emanated from within. Their consciousness expanded, merging with the raw power and serenity of the surroundings.

As Jai sank deeper into their meditation, the boundaries of their physical form seemed to dissolve. Their consciousness expanded beyond the limitations of their body, merging with the vastness of the universe. They felt an overwhelming sense of peace and connectedness.

In this heightened state of awareness, Jai became an observer of their own being. From a transcendent vantage point, they watched as their physical form sat serenely at the base of the waterfall, completely immersed in the present moment.

As Jai watched themselves in this state of deep meditation, a wave of understanding washed over them. They realized that this out-of-body experience was a glimpse of the infinite possibilities that lay within the realm of their own consciousness.

Eyes closed, Jai embraced the tranquility of their meditative state. Amidst the symphony of nature's whispers, a faint sound reached their ears. It was a sound unlike any other, delicate yet distinct—a soft whoosh accompanied by a hint of wings brushing through the air.

Intrigued by this ethereal sound, Jai's intuition sparked, urging them to open their eyes. As their eyelids fluttered open, their gaze was immediately drawn to a scene of wonder unfolding before them. With breathtaking precision, a dog, as if descending from the heavens, plummeted through the air and crashed into the water at the base of the falls.

Time seemed to slow down as Jai beheld this extraordinary sight. The dog's descent was both awe-inspiring and perilous, its body arcing through the air before disappearing beneath the surface. Concern and compassion welled up within Jai, compelling them to take action.

In a swift and decisive movement, Jai sprang into motion. Without hesitation, they hurried to the edge of the water, their heart pounding with a mixture of fear and determination. The sound of rushing water filled their ears as they surveyed the scene, their eyes locked on the spot where the dog had disappeared.

With an unwavering resolve, Jai entered the water, wading through the shallows towards the dog's anticipated location. The current tugged at their legs, but their focus remained unwavering. They knew that time was of the essence, and every passing moment heightened their concern for the dog's well-being.

As Jai neared the spot, anticipation and worry gripped their heart. And then, amidst the swirling currents, a figure emerged. It was the dog, drenched and disoriented, but miraculously alive. Jai's heart swelled with relief, their own weariness momentarily forgotten.

With gentle hands, Jai cradled the dog, offering reassurance and comfort. The water cascaded off their bodies, merging with the natural rhythm of the falls. Together, Jai and the dog made their way to the safety of the shore, where the tumultuous waters gave way to calm.

Exhausted but grateful, Jai knelt on the shore, still holding the dog close. Their eyes met, and in that instant, an unspoken connection formed. It was a bond forged through the shared experience of survival and the recognition of a shared path.

As Jai held the dog close, their gaze was drawn towards the cliff where sunlight bathed the surroundings in a breathtaking display of shimmering light. The rays danced upon the cascading water, creating a spectacle of natural beauty. The serene and ethereal ambiance enveloped Jai's senses, evoking a profound sense of wonder and tranquility.

Enraptured by the enchanting scene, Jai felt a deep resonance within their being. It was in that moment, amidst the shimmering light and the sound of flowing water, that the name "Kiran" sprang to Jai's mind and slipped from their lips.

"Kiran," Jai whispered, their voice resonating with appreciation and admiration for the beauty that surrounded them.

As Jai and Kiran sat by the small campfire, the crackling of the flames pierced the stillness of the night. The gentle glow cast flickering shadows, creating a serene ambiance that encouraged reflection and introspection. In the quietude of the moment, Jai's thoughts unraveled, and they felt compelled to share their recent profound experience with Kiran.

"Kiran," Jai began, their words blending with the gentle crackle of the fire, "during my meditation earlier, something extraordinary happened. I found myself in a state of deep stillness, and in that stillness, I had an out-of-body experience. I saw myself, as if I was watching from a distance."

The night seemed to hold its breath, and a pause lingered in the air as Jai's words settled. They sat quietly, their eyes reflecting the flickering firelight, lost in the contemplation of their own revelation. And then, a smile tugged at the corners of Jai's lips.

"But as I reflected on that experience," Jai continued, their voice tinged with a hint of amusement, "I couldn't help but realize the comical aspect of it all. If I was watching myself, then who was the one doing the watching? Why wasn't I watching myself watch myself?"

A moment of lightheartedness washed over Jai as they recognized the limitations of their imagination. They understood that true meditation was not about indulging in daydreams or illusions but rather about diving into the depths of their own consciousness, beyond the realm of mere imagination.

With a chuckle, Jai turned to Kiran, their eyes twinkling with newfound understanding. "You see, Kiran, I have come to realize that true meditation is about letting go of the illusions and distractions of the mind. It is about being fully present in the here and now, rather than getting lost in the play of our own thoughts and visions."

136

Jai closed their eyes, ready to immerse themselves in the serenity of meditation. They focused on their breath, allowing it to become their anchor in the present moment. With each inhale and exhale, they felt a deepening sense of peace and stillness washing over them.

But just as Jai started to settle into this tranquil state, a wet sensation brushed against their cheek. Startled, Jai opened their eyes to find Kiran's playful face inches away, a mischievous glimmer in their eyes. Before Jai could react, Kiran's tongue darted out, giving Jai's face an affectionate lick.

Jai couldn't help but burst into laughter, their peaceful meditation interrupted by Kiran's unexpected display of affection. "Kiran, my friend!" Jai exclaimed, still chuckling. "I'm trying to be in the moment here."

Kiran wagged their tail enthusiastically, clearly delighted by the reaction they had elicited. They continued to shower Jai with more licks, their tail wagging with unrestrained joy.

Amidst the laughter and the slobbery kisses, Jai couldn't help but feel a deep sense of gratitude for Kiran's presence. They realized that even in the pursuit of inner stillness, life's little interruptions and unexpected moments of connection were valuable reminders of the beauty and unpredictability of the present moment.

PART THREE – CHAPTER TWO
Gramani Rajendra awakening

As the first rays of sunlight painted the sky in hues of gold, Gramani Rajendra stirred from his slumber. He rose with purpose, the weight of his responsibilities settling upon his shoulders. For he was the Gramani, the village leader, entrusted with the welfare and guidance of his people.

Gramani Rajendra's role in the community was one of authority and power. He was responsible for upholding the laws, resolving disputes, and ensuring the harmony and prosperity of the village. His voice held weight, his decisions carried consequences, and his presence commanded respect.

Each day, Gramani Rajendra meticulously prepared himself to face the challenges that awaited him. He adorned himself in garments that symbolized his authority, adjusting his regal robe with precision. As he looked into the mirror, he couldn't help but feel a pang of loneliness deep within his heart.

Gazing at his reflection, Gramani Rajendra saw a man burdened by the weight of his responsibilities. The lines on his face told stories of countless nights spent worrying and strategizing for the village's welfare. But beneath the façade of strength, doubts lingered, like shadows in the corners of his mind.

In a moment of vulnerability, he whispered to himself, "I am Rajendra, a strong and powerful Gramani." The words echoed in the stillness of the room, an affirmation meant to drown out the insecurities that threatened to surface. He fought against the loneliness that often accompanied his position, seeking solace in the image he projected to the world.

But no matter how resolute his voice, the emptiness persisted. The longing for genuine connection and understanding tugged at his soul, hidden behind the stoic mask he wore for the villagers. Gramani Rajendra yearned for companionship, someone who could see beyond the facade and appreciate the vulnerable man beneath.

With a heavy sigh, he composed himself, forcing a smile upon his face. He steeled his resolve and reminded himself of the role he must play in the village. The Gramani had to be a pillar of strength, unwavering and invulnerable. The loneliness he felt would be swept aside, buried deep within his heart, as he carried out his duties with unwavering determination.

Leaving the mirror behind, Gramani Rajendra stepped out of his chamber and into the village. The villagers greeted him respectfully, their eyes filled with admiration for the powerful leader they perceived him to be. And while their reverence warmed his heart, the emptiness within still gnawed at his soul.

As Gramani Rajendra walked through the village, his presence commanded attention. The villagers would hush their conversations, their voices growing softer as he passed. The children, full of energy and laughter, would slow their running and give him respectful nods. Even the drunk lying in the streets would scramble to find some semblance of sobriety in his presence, hastily getting up and shuffling away.

Feeling a glimmer of confidence, Rajendra noticed a beautiful woman standing nearby. Intrigued, he approached her with the intention of starting a conversation. However, before he could utter a word, she cut him off with a firm but polite response.

"We're not doing anything," she said, her voice carrying a hint of frustration. "We're just standing here. Go ruin someone else's day."

Surprised and taken aback by her words, Rajendra stood there momentarily, his heart sinking. It was as if the woman saw through his façade, exposing his insecurities with a simple sentence. He watched as she swiftly turned and walked away, leaving him feeling a mix of embarrassment and longing for connection.

In that moment, Gramani Rajendra took a deep breath, regaining his composure. He repeated to himself, "I am Rajendra, a strong and powerful Gramani." Determined to overcome his doubts, he straightened his posture, pushing away the sting of rejection, and continued his journey through the village, ready to face the challenges that lay ahead.

As Gramani Rajendra walked through the village, he was captivated by the enchanting melodies of the Veena that filled the air. The Veena player skillfully plucked the strings, their fingers dancing across the instrument, weaving a tapestry of music that resonated deeply within Gramani Rajendra's being. He was uplifted by the soulful tunes, feeling a sense of joy and inner peace wash over him.

Filled with gratitude, Gramani Rajendra eagerly waited for the music to reach its final notes, intending to express his appreciation to the talented performer. However, as the last strains of the Veena echoed through the village, the street performer swiftly gathered their belongings, a look of fear and apprehension etched on their face. Misinterpreting

Gramani Rajendra's presence as a sign of trouble, they hastily fled the scene, leaving him standing there, his heart sinking further.

In that moment, Gramani Rajendra couldn't help but question his role in the village and the impact he had on those around him. Despite his intentions to enforce order and maintain harmony, it seemed that his presence instilled fear and caused people to retreat. Doubt crept into his mind, casting shadows on his self-perception.

But he refused to let these doubts consume him. With a deep breath, he straightened his posture and whispered to himself, "I am Rajendra, a strong and powerful Gramani. I have a responsibility to protect and guide my community."

Gramani Rajendra's gaze fell upon a person sitting on the ground, accompanied by a dog. The person's eyes were closed, their face serene and peaceful. Intrigued, Gramani Rajendra observed from a distance, captivated by the aura of calmness that surrounded them. It was as if a gentle radiance emanated from the person, drawing him closer.

Reluctant to disturb the tranquil scene, Gramani Rajendra hesitated for a moment. But his curiosity and longing for connection urged him forward. With measured steps, he approached the person, mustering up the courage to break their meditation. As he reached their side, he greeted them with utmost politeness and respect.

To his surprise, the person opened their eyes, their countenance brightening with a warm smile. They reciprocated the greeting, acknowledging Gramani Rajendra's presence with kindness and openness. Intrigued by the person's demeanor, he couldn't help but inquire about their activity.

"What is it that you are doing?" Gramani Rajendra inquired, his voice filled with genuine curiosity.

With a gentle smile, the person responded, "I am meditating. It is a practice that allows me to cultivate inner peace, clarity, and connection with myself and the world around me."

Gramani Rajendra, filled with curiosity and a hint of frustration, asks Jai, "Who are you? What do you do?"

Jai calmly replies, "I am Jai."

Perplexed, Gramani Rajendra insists, "No, no, no. Not your name. Who are you? What is your purpose?" Jai responds with a serene smile, "I am Jai. I am simply being myself."

Growing increasingly agitated, Gramani Rajendra raises his voice, "I am Gramani Rajendra, a powerful and respected leader of this village. Who are you?"

With unwavering composure, Jai replies, "I am Jai. I apologize for the confusion. I meditate, practice yoga, and embark on adventures in nature. This is my dog, Kiran. Kiran doesn't speak much, do you, Kiran?" Jai looks at Kiran and chuckles softly.

Gramani Rajendra dismisses Kiran's silence, exclaiming, "That's because it's a dog! But who are you?"

Remaining calm, Jai replies, "I am a person. In this life, I am on a quest to find the Moksha Vriksha tree. In past lives, I was a scholar, an educator, and a spouse of an artisan. But those are all illusions, my friend. I am not defined by those roles. I am simply Jai. Who are you?"

Overwhelmed with emotion, Gramani Rajendra's tough exterior crumbles, and tears stream down his face. In that moment, he begins to question his own identity and purpose, realizing the hollowness that lies within.

Jai, understanding Gramani Rajendra's struggle, places a gentle hand on his shoulder and says, "Don't despair, Rajendra. Your true essence goes beyond your title. Take a moment to breathe, to embrace your vulnerabilities, and to rediscover the depths of your being."

Moved by Jai's words, Gramani Rajendra wipes away his tears and takes a deep breath. He gathers his composure and says, "I am... myself."

Jai smiles warmly and nods, "Yes, yes you are, my friend. Embrace the power and authenticity that lies within you. Remember, true strength is found in vulnerability and self-awareness."

With a newfound sense of purpose and a glimmer of hope in his eyes, Gramani Rajendra thanks Jai for his guidance. The two part ways, each on their own path of self-discovery.

Gramani Rajendra, fueled by a newfound sense of joy and liberation, runs through the village in search of the Veena player. His heart beats with anticipation as he follows the sound of enchanting music to a quiet side street. There, he finds the Veena player, their fingers gracefully plucking the strings, weaving a mesmerizing melody.

Without hesitation, Gramani Rajendra removes his regal robe, casting away the weight of his title. He starts to sway to the rhythm, his body moving in synchrony with the music. The Veena player's eyes widen in surprise, but a smile slowly spreads across their face. They join the impromptu dance, their music blending with the beats of Gramani Rajendra's steps.

As if by magic, the villagers are drawn to the scene. The once-timid woman, whose words had stung Gramani Rajendra earlier, now smiles and joins the dance. The children, who had slowed their playful run in his presence, giggle with delight and twirl around him. The village comes alive with a celebration of movement and joy.

In the midst of the village celebration, two children, Aanya and Dev, observed from a distance.

144

"Look at Gramani Rajendra!" Dev whispered. "He's... different."

Aanya nodded, "He's just being himself."

"But isn't that hard sometimes?" Dev asked.

Aanya smiled, "Maybe, but look how happy he is."

With that, the two joined the dance, their laughter mingling with the village's joy.

In that moment, Gramani Rajendra realizes the power of connection and the beauty of embracing his true self. He dances with abandon, his worries and self-consciousness dissolving into the rhythm of the music. The weight of his authority is replaced by a sense of unity, as if every step he takes brings him closer to the heart of his community.

Jai and Kiran, their journey continuing beyond the village, observe the transformation with a knowing smile. They understand that their encounter with Gramani Rajendra has sparked a profound change within him. With the village now immersed in the dance of life, Jai and Kiran bid farewell, continuing their quest to find the elusive Moksha Vriksha tree.

PART THREE - CHAPTER THREE
Embers of Remembrance

Jai and Kiran continued their journey through the lush forest, their spirits lifted by the serenity of their surroundings. The sunlight filtered through the dense canopy above, casting a warm, golden glow on their path. With each step, they felt a sense of connection to nature, embracing the tranquility that enveloped them.

As evening approached, Jai found a cozy spot amidst the trees to set up camp. The crackling fire added a comforting warmth to the cool evening air. Jai unpacked their supplies, carefully selecting a collection of leaves and herbs gathered along their journey.

With a gentle touch, Jai began to prepare a soothing tea, the aroma of the herbs mingling with the earthy scent of the forest. Kiran, ever curious, watched intently, their tail wagging in anticipation. Jai's hands moved with grace and familiarity, instinctively knowing the right proportions and combinations.

The flames danced in the fire pit, casting flickering shadows that seemed to merge with the surrounding trees. Jai's heart felt light, a sense of wonder filling their being. They poured hot water into the pot, allowing the mixture to steep and infuse, releasing its essence.

As Jai took a sip from the clay cup, the flavors danced on their tongue, carrying a hint of bitterness that soon gave way to a subtle sweetness. The warmth of the tea spread throughout Jai's body, comforting and calming their senses.

Sitting beside the crackling fire, Jai felt a gentle buzz of anticipation building within. The forest seemed to come alive with vibrant energy, every rustle of leaves and chirping of birds resonating with newfound clarity. The boundaries between Jai and the natural world blurred, as if they were merging with the very essence of the forest itself.

With each sip, the tea worked its magic, unlocking hidden chambers within Jai's mind and heart. Colors grew more vibrant, sounds more melodious, and time itself seemed to stretch and contract in a symphony of sensory perception.

As Jai's senses soared in the kaleidoscope of perception, they turned their gaze to Kiran, their faithful companion. In that altered state, the boundaries between human and canine dissolved, and Jai felt a profound connection with Kiran, as if the dog could speak their thoughts.

Jai's eyes met Kiran's soulful gaze, and in the depths of their mind, a conversation unfolded. The crackling fire provided the backdrop for their mystical exchange.

"Jai," Kiran began, their voice resonating within Jai's consciousness, "do you see the fire? Its dance is a mesmerizing spectacle, weaving tales of life's mysteries."

Jai, amazed by Kiran's apparent ability to speak, nodded eagerly. "Yes, Kiran, I see it. The fire is like a majestic performer, captivating us with its graceful movements. It possesses a power that both fascinates and humbles."

Kiran continued, their voice carrying wisdom beyond their doggy form. "Indeed, Jai. The fire embodies the essence of transformation. Just as it engulfs and consumes, it also offers warmth and light. It is a symbol of renewal, a reminder that from the ashes, new beginnings can emerge."

Jai's mind absorbed Kiran's words, feeling a sense of solace and understanding. In this altered state, the conversation with their loyal companion became a channel to explore their innermost thoughts and emotions.

"Kiran, my dear friend," Jai responded, their voice filled with awe, "the fire's dance mirrors the complexities of our own lives. It reminds us that even in our darkest moments, there is a flicker of hope, a chance for redemption."

Kiran wagged their tail with excitement and playfully barked, "Hey Jai, what did one flame say to the other? 'You're on fire today!' Get it? Because flames are always burning brightly!"

Jai chuckled, their laughter blending with the crackling of the campfire. "Oh, Kiran, you always know how to bring warmth and humor to any moment. You truly light up my world, my faithful friend."

Kiran's tail wagged vigorously as they couldn't contain their excitement for another joke. They barked gleefully, "Jai, here's another one for you! What's a fire's favorite type of music? 'Hot' hits! Because, you know, fire is hot and music can be a hit!"

Jai burst into laughter. "Oh, Kiran, you really know how to spark a smile in my heart. Your sense of humor is truly a blaze of joy."

As the flames danced and swayed, painting a mesmerizing picture against the night sky, Jai and Kiran continued their lighthearted conversation. The warmth of the fire seemed to echo the warmth of their bond, creating a comforting and inviting ambiance in the midst of their journey.

Jai's laughter began to subside, and their gaze shifted to the fire dancing before them. The flames flickered and swayed, casting a mesmerizing glow that illuminated the surrounding darkness. As their eyes traced the intricate patterns of the fire's dance, a sudden realization dawned upon them—the tea they had consumed was none other than soma, the mystical plant of profound significance.

A wave of awe washed over Jai, their breath catching in their throat. The cup, once innocently held in their hands, now held a sacred elixir that had the power to transcend ordinary boundaries. The air around them seemed to thicken with reverence as they comprehended the magnitude of what they had ingested.

As Jai's mind delved deeper into the realms of the soma's influence, a surge of ancient knowledge coursed through their veins. The fragments of memories and scholarly wisdom pieced together like a long-lost puzzle, revealing a hidden truth that had remained concealed within their being.

In the flickering glow of the fire, Jai's gaze turned inward, navigating the labyrinthine corridors of their consciousness. As they retraced the paths of their past, the image of a scholar emerged—a figure dedicated to unraveling the secrets of the natural world, including the mystical properties of soma.

A profound realization washed over Jai, like a cleansing tide eroding the walls of denial that had guarded their memories. They had been an educator, a dispenser of wisdom and knowledge. Their pursuit of truth had led them to dive deep into the mysteries of plants, unearthing the transformative powers hidden within them.

As Jai gazed into the mesmerizing dance of the flames, a vivid vision pierced through the veil of their consciousness. The crackling fire took on a menacing hue, casting eerie shadows that seemed to morph into haunting shapes. The scent of smoke filled their nostrils, triggering a surge of memories from the depths of their being.

In the midst of the inferno, a figure emerged, ethereal and engulfed in flickering embers. It was Mata, their beloved significant other, standing amidst the engulfing flames. The intensity of the hallucination gripped Jai's heart, evoking a primal surge of anguish and fear.

The tendrils of smoke twisted and coiled, whispering haunting echoes of the past. Jai's mind struggled to reconcile the truth—the devastating fire that had consumed their dwelling and claimed Mata's life. The guilt that had burdened their soul now surged forth with an unrelenting force, threatening to consume them from within.

Tears welled up in Jai's eyes as they witnessed the spectral image of Mata, their heart wrenching with a maelstrom of grief and regret. The flickering fire became an agonizing reminder of their absence during that fateful event, a wound that had festered in their soul.

The hallucination played out like a tortured dance, Mata's form contorted by the twisting flames, their eyes filled with a mix of accusation and longing. It was a haunting reminder of the price paid for Jai's absence, a piercing lament that echoed through the depths of their consciousness.

In that moment of despair, Jai's trembling hands reached into their pocket, instinctively grasping for solace. And there it was—a folded palm leaf, worn and creased with the passage of time. Carefully, they unfurled it, revealing a handwritten poem, Mata's loving gift, bestowed upon Jai before their ill-fated departure.

With blurred vision, Jai read the delicate words etched upon the parchment. The poem was an embodiment of Mata's soul—a testament to their love, a gentle reminder of the beauty they shared. The verses caressed Jai's wounded spirit, providing a balm for their tormented soul.

In the boundless tapestry of time and space,
Our souls entwined in an eternal embrace.
A symphony of love, a dance of hearts,
United forever, never to be apart.

Like gentle whispers carried by the breeze,
Our love transcends all boundaries with ease.
In your eyes, I find solace and grace,
A sanctuary where my spirit finds its place.

Through life's vast labyrinth, we've journeyed as one,
Navigating the tides, basking in the sun.
Hand in hand, we've faced both joy and sorrow,
Braving the storms, building a brighter tomorrow.

Your laughter, a melody that fills the air,
Paints vibrant colors, banishes despair.
With every touch, a universe awakes,
Igniting passions that no darkness can break.

We are the rivers, merging in perfect flow,
Where depths of love and understanding grow.
Our essence interwoven, an eternal song,
A love that's boundless, enduring, and strong.

Though fate's winds may scatter us afar,
Know that our love transcends every star.
For in the realm of the heart, we forever reside,
A love immortal, where all barriers subside.

Let this ode echo through the ages to come,
A tribute to a love that's never undone.
In each word and line, our souls intertwined,
A love eternal, forever enshrined.

May this poem be a reminder, my love,
Of the infinite blessings that flow from above.
In this world and beyond, we're destined to be,
Forever connected, in love's symphony.

PART THREE - CHAPTER 0

Mirrored Flames: Clearing Forgiveness

As the wheels of the cart rattled along the dusty road, Jai's heart swelled with anticipation. It had been weeks since their departure, engrossed in their scholarly pursuits, and now they were finally on their way back home. Thoughts of Mata filled their mind, a beacon of love and warmth in the midst of their travels.

As the familiar landscape came into view, Jai's excitement grew, but a sense of unease lingered in the air. Something felt off, out of place. The closer they got to their dwelling, the heavier their heart became, as if weighed down by an invisible burden.

And then, Jai saw it—a haunting sight that shattered their world. Where once stood their beloved home, now lay a pile of charred rubble, its blackened remains whispering tales of devastation and loss. The air hung heavy with the scent of burnt wood and lingering sorrow.

Neighbors, their faces etched with empathy, gathered around the ruins, offering silent gestures of support. But Jai's gaze remained fixed on the fragments of their life, searching for any trace of what once was. Among the debris, they spotted fragments of Mata's cherished artworks, fragments that held memories of beauty and creativity.

With a mixture of despair and determination, Jai began salvaging what they could. A fragile satchel, once filled with dreams and aspirations, now held the remnants of their shared life. As Jai clutched it tightly, a flicker of hope ignited within, refusing to be extinguished by the ashes of the past.

In the midst of the chaos, Jai's gaze caught the reflection of the mirror, encrusted with a layer of dust. Intrigued, they reached out and wiped away the grime, revealing their own reflection staring back at them—a fragmented image, distorted by the trials and tribulations of their journey.

But as their eyes met their own gaze, a conversation began—a dialogue that transcended the confines of the physical world. Jai spoke to the reflection of Mata in the mirror, pouring out their heart, apologizing with desperate fervor for not being there, for the pain they felt deep within.

"Oh, Mata, my love," Jai's voice quivered with emotion, "I'm sorry, so deeply sorry for not being there, for not protecting you from this tragedy. I carry the weight of this guilt, this burden of not being able to save what we held dear."

The reflection of Mata in the mirror remained silent, a mere image that mirrored Jai's pain and regret. Jai continued, their voice filled with a mixture of remorse and longing.

"I can't help but wonder what I could have done differently. If only I had been there, if only I had awakened to the danger before it was too late. I would have given my own life to protect you, to ensure your safety."

Jai's words hung in the air, filling the space between reality and memory. They stared at Mata's reflection, searching for solace and forgiveness. The mirror, still and unyielding, absorbed their words, holding a reflection of their own sorrow.

Tears welled up in Jai's eyes as they pleaded, "Mata, please forgive me. I loved you with all my heart, and I failed to shield you from harm. The pain of your absence is unbearable, and I can't escape the guilt that gnaws at my soul."

The reflection in the mirror remained unchanged, a silent witness to Jai's heartfelt confession. Jai's voice cracked with emotion as they continued to speak, their words pouring out like a torrent of emotions.

"I know I can't change the past, but I want you to know that you were my everything. Your art, your poetry, your smile, your love, your presence—I cherished it all. Losing you has left an emptiness within me that no words can describe."

Jai reached out, their fingers tracing the outline of Mata's reflection, as if trying to bridge the gap between the physical and the ethereal. Their voice, now a whisper, trembled with vulnerability.

"Mata, please know that I will always love you. Though you may be gone, your spirit lives on within me. I will honor your memory by finding the strength to heal and carry your love forward into the world."

As Jai's words faded, a fragile moment of silence enveloped them. The reflection of Mata in the mirror remained motionless, a poignant reminder of the irreparable loss. But something within Jai urged them to go further, to seek a deeper understanding.

In that profound moment of self-recognition, the conversation transformed. Jai's voice, still filled with vulnerability, shifted towards a dialogue of self-discovery and self-forgiveness.

"I have carried this guilt for so long, blaming myself for the fire, for not being there to protect you, Mata," Jai spoke, their voice laced with a mix of sorrow and determination. "But perhaps I have been looking in the wrong direction for forgiveness. It is not your forgiveness I seek, but my own."

The reflection seemed to nod in understanding, a glimmer of compassion shining through their eyes. Jai continued; their words filled with newfound clarity.

"I let my memories of us be tainted by the pain of our loss. I have carried the weight of the past, of what could have been, for far too long. But I realize now that dwelling in guilt and regret only keeps me chained to that painful moment. I must find a way to release myself from this burden, to embrace healing and honor our love."

As Jai's gaze remained fixed on their reflection, they spoke with a newfound sense of acceptance and self-compassion. "Mata, I cannot change what has happened, but I can change how I carry your memory within me. Instead of allowing guilt to consume me, I will choose to honor you by living a life filled with love, kindness, and creativity. I will carry your essence forward, weaving it into the fabric of my being."

Jai's words hung in the air, a resolute declaration of their intentions. The reflection in the mirror seemed to glow with a gentle warmth, as if offering a silent affirmation.

With a steadying breath, Jai made a final vow to themselves, to Mata, and to the universe that surrounded them.

"I will no longer be defined by the ashes of our past. Instead, I will rise from them. I will embrace the beauty that still exists in the world, in memories and in new connections. I will find solace in knowing that your love will forever guide me, even as I navigate this journey alone."

Jai wiped away the remaining dust from the mirror, their own reflection stood before them—unblemished, resilient, and filled with the potential for growth. It was a moment of profound self-realization, an acknowledgment of their own strength and capacity for healing.

As Jai's own reflection leaned forward, transcending the boundaries of the mirror, a mix of surprise and bewilderment washed over them.

Before Jai could comprehend the surreal scene unfolding before their eyes, their reflection's tongue gently brushed against their cheek, leaving a moist and unexpected sensation.

"What are you doing?" Jai asked, their voice filled with both confusion and curiosity. Yet, their reflection repeated the action, licking Jai's face once more. It was an intimate gesture, a reminder of connection and playfulness, yet also an enigma.

Before Jai could delve further into the mysterious encounter, their consciousness flickered, and the dream realm dissipated. Jai's eyes fluttered open, greeted by the warm morning sunlight filtering through the trees.

The campfire, once ablaze with vibrant flames, had now dwindled to embers, leaving behind a serene stillness. To Jai's surprise, it was not their own reflection that had kissed their cheek, but rather their loyal companion, Kiran, their furry friend who had awakened them from the depths of their dream. Kiran's tail wagged excitedly, their eyes brimming with joy and an eagerness to start the day.

Chuckling softly, Jai sat up and embraced Kiran, their faithful companion. The remnants of the dream lingered, still fresh in their mind, but now accompanied by a newfound sense of comfort and acceptance.

The fire may have been extinguished, but within Jai's heart, a new flame had ignited—a flame of self-discovery, self-forgiveness, and a rekindled spirit.

As Kiran licked tears from Jai's cheek, they realized that healing and growth were not solitary endeavors but intertwined with the love and support of those around them, both human and canine.

The morning unfolded as Jai and Kiran embarked on a new day. Hand in paw, they ventured forth, their hearts resonating with a deep sense of purpose. The challenges and blessings that lay ahead seemed insignificant in the face of the transformation they had already begun.

The ashes of the past no longer held them captive, for Jai had discovered the power within to rise above the embers of sorrow and forge a path towards wholeness. And Kiran, their faithful companion, served as a constant reminder of the unwavering love and resilience that resided within them both.

Together, they ventured towards a destination shrouded in mystique– the Moksha Vriksha. They were guided by an unwavering belief that within the embrace of the tree, they would discover the key to healing and liberation.

PART THREE -
CHAPTER FIVE
Liberating Laughter and Sunlit Paths

As Jai and Kiran continued their challenging journey towards the sacred Moksha Vriksha tree, they encountered a heavy downpour during their sleep. The relentless rain poured down, saturating the earth and transforming the once-moist soil into a treacherous quagmire.

When Jai and Kiran woke up, they found themselves trapped in the muddy ground. The rain had turned the terrain into a sticky, mire-like substance that clung to their feet and paws, impeding their movement. Each step became a struggle as they fought against the suction-like force of the mud.

Their frustration grew as they tried to break free, but their efforts only seemed to deepen their entrapment. Jai's feet sank deeper into the muck, while Kiran's paws were firmly stuck, making it nearly impossible for them to escape.

Realizing the futility of their initial struggle, Jai took a moment to gather their thoughts and emotions. With a deep breath, they shifted their mindset from resistance to acceptance. They understood that forcing their way out of the mud would only lead to further entanglement.

In this moment of clarity, Jai reached out and gently stroked Kiran's fur, conveying a silent message of reassurance and solidarity. Kiran, sensing Jai's change in demeanor, leaned into the touch, finding comfort in the unspoken bond between them.

Together, they embraced the stillness of the situation, waiting patiently for a shift in circumstances. They understood that nature's elements could be unpredictable, and sometimes, the best course of action was to allow time and the forces of nature to guide their liberation.

As they sat there, trapped but not defeated, a renewed sense of resilience and determination began to emerge within Jai and Kiran. They knew that this challenge was just a temporary setback in their grand journey towards the Moksha Vriksha tree.

In the midst of their contemplation, Jai's playful spirit sparked a memory. They turned to Kiran with a warm smile and began to share a story, diverting their attention from their current predicament. Jai began to speak, their voice filled with a playful tone. "Kiran, my dear friend, let me narrate to you a legend from the ancient valleys of the Indus. It speaks of a cow—no ordinary cow. This one had an odd quirk; it perceived everything as if reflected in a mirror."

Kiran's gaze locked onto Jai, intrigued and waiting for more. Jai went on, "Determined to overcome this hurdle, the resilient cow journeyed through educational halls, hoping to gain knowledge and a solution to its mirrored vision."

Kiran's tail moved in excitement as Jai depicted the cow's challenges. A cheeky inflection colored Jai's voice as they approached the tale's zenith.

"One fateful day, the cow, mustering the loudest cry it could, caused something extraordinary," Jai related, their eyes shining with merriment.

"Attracted by the unusual sound, sages and spiritualists gathered in the meadows where the cow roamed."

Sensing Jai's excitement, Kiran's ears stood at attention. Jai took a dramatic pause, savoring the anticipation, then joyously delivered the twist. "And the sound the cow made, dearest Kiran? It bellowed 'Ohm'!"

Jai's laughter echoed, thoroughly enjoying the jest of the cow's condition. Picking up on Jai's delight, Kiran chimed in with cheerful barks and a swishing tail.

"Do you grasp, Kiran, why the cow's call was 'Ohm'? When attempting 'Moo', the inverse was 'Ohm'!"

Their laughter filled the air, mingling with the serene ambiance of the natural surroundings. Jai, still chuckling, continued their storytelling spree, unable to contain their playful spirit.

"Kiran, I have a friend who opened a magnificent space for everyone to come together and practice meditation. My friend wanted to attract people to this special place, so they came up with a brilliant idea. They put a sign on the door of the space, and you know what it said?" Jai paused, waiting for Kiran's response, their tail wagging in anticipation.

Kiran looked at Jai with their soulful eyes, their head again tilting slightly to one side.

The sign said, 'Inquire within!'" Jai exclaimed between bursts of laughter, their voice carrying a hint of mischief. Kiran, though unable to fully grasp the words, wagged their tail in response to the contagious joy radiating from their companion.

Amidst their shared amusement, Jai managed to catch their breath and continued, "You know, Kiran, in meditation, there's a lot of inner work and self-reflection. So, my friend cleverly wanted to convey the idea of looking within ourselves. But, they also wanted people to ask about the new space! It's a play on words, isn't it?" Jai chuckled, finding the humor in the double entendre.

Amidst fits of laughter, Jai shared another tale, "Have I ever told you about the time I witnessed a wise sage ordering at the bustling market? The kind cook asked, 'What can I make for you?' and the sage replied, 'Make me one with everything, please!'"

Jai's laughter echoed through the air, blending with the rustling leaves and the distant chirping of birds. Kiran, although unable to grasp the intricacies of the joke, found sheer joy in their companion's infectious mirth. Their wagging tail and bright eyes were testament to the unspoken connection they shared.

As their laughter gradually subsided, Jai and Kiran basked in the serenity of the moment. The rain, which had once trapped them in the muddy ground, now started to recede, and a gentle warmth spread through the air as the sun peeked through the clouds. Its golden rays caressed the earth, slowly drying the mud that had held them captive.

With each passing moment, the sun's radiant touch worked its magic, transforming the once-muddy ground into a firm and walkable path. Jai and Kiran felt the clay beneath their feet gradually lose its grip, allowing them to break free from their temporary prison.

Jai and Kiran traversed the path with renewed vitality. The sun, now a constant companion in the vast sky, illuminated their way and warmed their spirits. The world around them seemed to echo their triumph, with nature's symphony providing a soundtrack of harmony and celebration.

PART THREE - CHAPTER FOUR
Embracing the Essence

As the days melted into one another, Jai and Kiran continued their journey along the winding path that led to the sacred Moksha Vriksha tree. Each step carried them further into the realm of self-discovery and inner transformation. They walked in sync with the rhythm of nature, their souls attuned to the subtle whispers of the universe.

Through dense forests and open meadows, they traveled, a harmonious duo in pursuit of spiritual awakening. The air was alive with the fragrance of wildflowers, and the sunlight filtered through the canopy, painting a kaleidoscope of colors upon the forest floor. Birds sang their melodic tunes, while gentle streams whispered secrets of ancient wisdom.

As twilight embraced the land, Jai gathered ingredients foraged along the journey and prepared a simple meal by the campfire. Each step was performed with intention, every movement an act of mindfulness.

Under the blanket of a starry sky, Jai and Kiran understood that every moment, approached with mindfulness and appreciation, could be transformed into a sacred experience, weaving their souls with the rhythm of the universe.

163

They climbed hills that kissed the heavens, their breath mingling with the crisp mountain air. Atop those peaks, they embraced the vastness of the world, feeling the pulsating energy of the universe beneath their feet.

They witnessed the majesty of sunrise and sunset, where the sky painted itself in hues of gold and crimson, reminding them of the ever-changing beauty of existence.

As they journeyed along the winding path, Jai and Kiran walked with mindfulness, each step a gentle connection to the earth. They breathed in the scents of the forest, the fragrance of wildflowers, and let the rhythm of their breath synchronize with the rhythm of nature.

With each inhalation, they welcomed clarity and peace into their beings, and with each exhalation, they released any tension or worries that weighed them down. Their breath became a mantra, a constant reminder to be fully present in the here and now.

In the embrace of nature, surrounded by the symphony of birdsong and rustling leaves, Jai and Kiran discovered the profound stillness that resides within. The world around them became a living meditation, a sanctuary of tranquility where they could nourish their spirits and find solace in the simplicity of being.

In this mindful walk, they found the sacredness in every step, every breath, and every moment, cultivating a deep sense of gratitude for the journey and the transformative power it held. And as they continued, hand in paw, they carried the essence of mindfulness with them, a guiding light illuminating their path to the Moksha Vriksha tree.

And then, one evening, as the sun began its descent towards the horizon, casting a warm glow upon the landscape, Jai and Kiran saw it—

the Moksha Vriksha tree. Its branches reached towards the heavens, adorned with leaves that shimmered like gold in the dying light. It stood as a symbol of wisdom and transcendence, beckoning them to draw closer.

But in that moment, as the world around them bathed in the glow of twilight, Jai and Kiran made a choice. They chose to sit, side by side, on a patch of soft grass, their eyes fixed upon the radiant spectacle before them. The colors of the sky danced in harmony with their souls, as if mirroring the vastness and beauty within.

They knew they had enough time to reach the tree, to complete their journey before night fall. But there was something captivating about this moment, a profound stillness that enveloped them. They surrendered to the grace of the fading sun, watching as it bid farewell to the day, while a gentle breeze whispered lullabies in their ears.

And as the sun dipped below the horizon, casting the world into the embrace of twilight, Jai and Kiran felt a deep sense of peace wash over them. In that tranquil space, they realized that sometimes the destination is not the ultimate goal, but the journey itself—a tapestry of experiences, emotions, and connections that shape the very essence of being.

PART THREE - CHAPTER SIX
The Key to Healing

As Jai stood before the magnificent Moksha Vriksha tree, a sense of awe and anticipation filled their heart. The tree, standing tall and majestic, emanated an aura of ancient wisdom and serenity. It was here, in the presence of this sacred symbol, that Jai's journey would reach a pivotal moment.

With trembling hands, Jai reached out and gently touched the rough bark of the tree. As if in response to their touch, a small key and a delicate chest materialized at the base of the tree. The key glimmered with an ethereal light, beckoning Jai to uncover its purpose.

Curiosity ignited within Jai's soul as they held the key in their hands, its intricate design glinting in the gentle light filtering through the tree's foliage. The weight of possibility hung in the air, as if the universe itself held its breath in anticipation of the revelation to come.

With cautious movements, Jai kneeled next to the small chest, its ornate carvings and delicate craftsmanship a testament to its sacred nature. The chest seemed to hold secrets of profound significance, whispering promises of profound understanding and enlightenment.

As the key slipped effortlessly into the lock, a sense of anticipation filled the air. With a gentle turn, the chest yielded, its lid lifting to unveil the treasures held within. But what Jai discovered within its depths was unexpected—an identical key, shimmering in harmonious resonance with the original.

A sense of wonder and astonishment washed over Jai, their eyes fixed upon the duplicate key. The realization dawned upon them like the first rays of sunlight breaking through a veil of clouds. It was not merely another key; it symbolized a profound truth—the key to healing lay not in a singular destination but in the ongoing journey itself.

The journey of liberation, Jai understood, was not a linear path leading to a fixed point of arrival. It was an ever-unfolding exploration, a perpetual dance between introspection and outward growth. Each step taken, each experience embraced, held the potential for profound transformation and self-discovery.

The keys became profound metaphors. They symbolized the interconnectedness of all beings on this shared journey of healing. It spoke of the collective wisdom passed down from those who had come before, who had traversed the path with courage and resilience. It was a testament to the wisdom that healing was a personal voyage, yet it resonated with the universal truths that bound humanity together.

With the duplicate key in their hand, Jai felt a surge of gratitude welling up within them—for the experiences that had shaped their being, for the love that had sustained them, and for the lessons learned along the way. It was a recognition that healing was not a solitary endeavor, but a tapestry woven with the threads of interconnectedness and compassion.

As Jai placed the duplicate key back into the chest, a sense of wholeness washed over them. They understood that the key to liberation was not simply about unlocking a single door, but about embracing the ongoing journey with open-hearted curiosity and a commitment to growth.

In that moment, a profound sense of purpose and determination enveloped Jai. They knew that their journey of healing would continue beyond the sacred confines of the Moksha Vriksha tree. It would extend into the vast expanse of their life, interweaving with the myriad experiences and encounters yet to come.

As the sun began its descent, casting a warm golden glow over the surroundings, Jai found a serene spot nearby to sit and reflect. The beauty of the moment enveloped them—the gentle rustling of leaves, the harmonious chorus of nature, and the soft whispers of their own breath. They surrendered to the present, immersing themselves in the essence of mindfulness.

But amidst the stillness, a wave of laughter suddenly welled up from deep within Jai's being. It started as a gentle chuckle, bubbling up like a playful brook, and soon transformed into an infectious, unbridled laughter that resonated through the tranquil setting. Jai's laughter echoed among the trees, blending with the chorus of nature.

With each peal of laughter, Jai felt an immense joy expanding within them. It was a laughter born out of sheer delight and amusement, a release of pent-up emotions that had been carried throughout their journey. They laughed at the irony of it all, at the cosmic dance of the universe.

In the midst of their laughter, Jai's mind wandered to the sage who had imparted the instructions, knowing full well that the key and chest lay nestled at the very bottom of the tree. They imagined the sage's mischievous grin, their eyes sparkling with wisdom and secret knowledge.

And then, Jai's laughter deepened as they imagined the countless brave souls who had stood in that very spot before them, their hearts brimming with hope and determination. They envisioned those who had discovered the key and chest, only to realize the profound truth that lay within. How they must have smiled, placed the key and chest back in their rightful place, and shared the legend of the tree with other brave seekers.

In the face of this realization, Jai's laughter became a celebration of shared humanity. The outward expression of joy acknowledged the interconnectedness of all those who had embarked on the journey of healing and self-discovery in the quest for liberation from burdens carried within. It was a laugh that celebrated the resilience and courage of the human spirit, and the inherent joy found in the continual pursuit of truth and enlightenment.

As Jai's laughter gradually subsided, a serene calmness washed over them. They gazed out into the horizon, the last rays of sunlight painting the sky with hues of orange and pink. The beauty of the moment lingered, merging with the joy that still resonated within Jai's being.

They knew that this laughter, this uncontainable joy, would remain etched in their memory, serving as a reminder of the transformative power of the journey they undertake. It was a laugh that symbolized the freedom and liberation found in embracing the path, rather than focusing solely on reaching a destination.

As the sun sank below the horizon and the world embraced the velvety darkness of night, Jai and Kiran found themselves nestled beneath the protective branches of a sprawling neem tree. They lay side by side, their eyes closed, breathing in harmony with the rhythm of the universe.

PART THREE - EPILOGUE
Bound by the Quest

"In the sweet embrace of oneness, the illusion of separation dissolves, and we realize our innate connection with all beings and the universe."

- Mata

As the scorching sun beat down on the dusty road, Jai sat in tranquil meditation beneath the sprawling neem tree. The morning breeze whispered through the leaves, carrying with it a sense of serenity and renewal. Next to Jai, Kiran, their faithful companion, observed the world with bright eyes, their presence a silent witness to the unfolding tale.

In the distance, a figure emerged, their steps faltering with weariness. The traveler approached with cautious determination, their gaze fixed upon Jai, sitting lost in deep contemplation. With weight of the world etched upon their weary face, the traveler sought solace in the presence of Jai.

Closing the distance, the traveler hesitated for a moment, their uncertainty palpable. With a silent understanding, Jai acknowledged their presence, silently inviting them to take a seat on the weathered rock nearby. The air seemed charged with anticipation, as if destiny had conspired to bring these two souls together.

Jai turned their head, their gaze meeting the traveler's eyes, mirroring the weariness and longing that resided within. There was a profound recognition, a silent acknowledgment of shared burdens and unspoken battles fought. It was as if the universe had orchestrated this meeting, a divine interplay of souls on a quest for solace and meaning.

"You seem burdened, my friend," Jai spoke softly, their voice carrying the weight of empathy. "The journey has not been kind to you, I see."

The traveler nodded, their eyes filled with a mix of pain and hope. "Indeed," they replied, their voice tinged with both exhaustion and determination. "The road has been treacherous, and I seek something... something that can heal the wounds within."

A gentle smile played upon Jai's lips, a reflection of deep understanding. "We are all travelers on this path of life," Jai murmured, their voice carrying the wisdom of countless stories. "Burdened by our own battles, seeking solace amidst the trials that shape us."

The traveler's gaze intensified, their curiosity kindling a flicker of anticipation. "Tell me, dear Jai," they whispered, their voice filled with longing. "Is there a way to find healing, a path that leads to restoration?"

Jai's eyes gleamed with ancient wisdom as they began to speak, their words weaving a tapestry of enchantment and wonder. They spoke of the Moksha Vriksha, the legendary tree said to hold the secrets of profound healing. Each word resonated with the universal yearning for transformation, the shared longing to find solace in the face of life's hardships.

As the traveler absorbed Jai's words, their heart quickened, its rhythm aligning with the pulse of the journey that awaited. They dared to imagine the winding paths, the treacherous terrain, and the whispers of ancient secrets that would accompany their every step. The yearning within bloomed into resolute determination, a flame that could not be extinguished.

"In the realms of existence," Jai continued, their voice a soothing melody, "we are but wanderers, seeking solace and a balm to soothe our wounds. The Moksha Vriksha beckons to us all, promising renewal and restoration."

In the hushed air, the traveler leaned closer, their eyes shimmering with curiosity. "Where can I find this sacred Moksha Vriksha?" they asked, their voice filled with anticipation and a tinge of longing.

Jai's gaze held a depth that transcended the physical realm, their voice carrying the echoes of countless journeys. "Listen closely, my dear traveler," they whispered, their words like a sacred incantation. "The path to the tree begins in the city of Mohendrapur. Seek out the seaweed alchemist and inquire about the story of Daya, the clownfish."

"I thank you, Jai, for your guidance," the traveler spoke, their voice filled with a mixture of gratitude and resolve. "I must continue on my path now, for the road ahead beckons me."

Jai nodded, their eyes shining with unwavering faith. "Go forth, brave seeker," they whispered, their voice carrying the weight of ancient blessings. "May the winds of destiny guide you, and may the tree unveil its secrets when the time is ripe."

Jai's gaze was drawn towards the sun, reflecting in the moment before finishing their sentiment. A touch of melancholy colored their features as they murmured, "... but not every dawn brings the same light."

The traveler embarked on their odyssey, guided by the whispers of ancient tales and the flickering light of hope. The path stretched before them, illuminated by the promise of transformation and renewal. They would navigate through darkness, embracing the challenges that tested their spirit, for within their very being lay the knowledge that true healing awaited, intricately woven into the fabric of the journey itself.

Kiran, filled with curiosity, turned their attention to Jai. Jai met their inquisitive eyes with a knowing smile. Sensing Kiran's unspoken question, Jai began to speak.

"We are each on our own journey," Jai explained, their voice gentle yet resolute. "The universe will guide the traveler to their own individual path, presenting challenges and opportunities that align with their unique needs and aspirations."

As Jai spoke, a wave of laughter began to bubbled up within them. With a mischievous twinkle in their eyes Jai continued, "The path begins with compassion. But you know, in reality, the Moksha Vriksha is only several hundred paces behind us."

Jai leaned in closer to Kiran, momentarily holding back their chuckle to whisper, "If the hermit told me where the tree was, if I had taken a quicker route, then I might never have met you."

As Jai's laughter gradually subsided, their gaze shifted behind them towards the Moksha Vriksha. They caught a glimpse of the majestic tree, its towering crown peeking above the dense canopy. A smile graced Jai's lips as they gleam into Kiran's eyes with understanding etched on their face.

"The answers we seek are often closer than we realize," Jai mused, their voice tinged with a hint of bittersweet wisdom. "But that doesn't make the journey any easier. It is through the challenges, the trials that test our spirit, that we find the strength to truly appreciate the beauty and significance of our quest."

Kiran, sensing the depth of their bond, inched closer to Jai. Their eyes locked, and in that silent exchange, a multitude of emotions swirled

174

— past, present, and future seemed to merge. There was a deep recognition, a fleeting glimpse of something ancient and eternal.

Jai's eyes held a shimmer of tears as they looked deeply into Kiran's. It was as if, for a split second, they saw more than just the loyal companion beside them. They saw a familiar soul, one that transcended lifetimes.

In the midst of their silent communion, a faint memory brushed Jai's consciousness — the soft whisper of Mata's voice, the warmth of their embrace, the depth of understanding they shared. It was gone in an instant, but the weight of it lingered.

Breaking the connection, Jai cleared their throat and chuckled softly, "Life has a funny way of guiding us, doesn't it? In seeking out one thing, we often find something else entirely. Or perhaps, rediscover something we once knew."

Kiran tilted their head, responding with a soft whine, eyes still fixed on Jai with unwavering trust and affection.

Jai took a deep breath, steadying themselves. "The universe holds its mysteries close," they mused, "but occasionally, if we're truly present, it grants us a brief glimpse into the grand tapestry of existence."

The two of them sat there, beneath the vast expanse of the sky, two souls bound by a journey that was more intricate and interconnected than they could possibly fathom.

Dear Reader,

Thank you for embarking on this journey with us. Your presence and engagement have been truly appreciated. We hope that the story we shared resonated with you in some way, offering moments of intrigue, reflection, or perhaps a brief escape from the ordinary.

If you enjoyed the book, we kindly ask you to consider sharing it with others who might find it intriguing or captivating. Your recommendation could introduce new readers to this world of imagination and discovery. Additionally, leaving a review or rating online would greatly support and encourage us as storytellers.

We sincerely hope that this book brought you some joy, entertainment, or a momentary respite from the everyday. Your support and enthusiasm mean the world to us.

Thank you once again for being a part of this journey. May your own adventures, both within the pages of books and in the moments of your life, continue to inspire and uplift you.

With Love,
   Nitka Marga

The Moksha Vriksha
Book Two

The
Sarvodaya Upavana

"The Sarvodaya Upavana"

In this captivating prequel to "The Moksha Vriksha," the narrative deepens as we follow Mata's journey into the realm of dreams. These are no ordinary dreams—Mata's experiences hold a hidden power that could reshape their reality.

As Mata explores the depths of their dreamscapes, they're not just a passenger but active participant, translating the whispers of the subconscious into vivid expressions of art and poetry. These aren't mere whims of the imagination but glimpses into concealed truths that blend past and future. Every piece of art and every poem becomes a key, unlocking layers of understanding that could reshape one's perception of the present.

Within the pages of this book, we join a multitude of brave seekers—1,000 in number—as they heed the call of a shared dream, all drawn to the mystical Sarvodaya Upavana. Here lies a shared destiny, a journey propelled by secrets that hold the very essence existence itself.

WWW.SOULBOUNDBOOKSINFO.COM

www.ingramcontent.com/pod-product-compliance
Lightning Source LLC
Chambersburg PA
CBHW050844180626

46814CB00007B/2618